PULLED IN

Rowena Dawn

Scarlet Leaf
2019

I0660332

Table of Contents

To Andreea and her soul mate

CHAPTER ONE

A DOOR SLAMMED HARD in the distance, and Darcy practically jumped out of her skin. She halted her furious pacing and sharpened her ears, listening intently.

Emmett Driscoll was in one of his moods. He barked orders left and right, but so fast that Darcy didn't understand what he was saying. The woman tiptoed to the door and listened intently.

Quick steps sounded on the wooden floors toward the front exit of the mansion. Darcy sighed with relief, leaned her shoulders on the door, and crossed her arms over her chest. Emmett didn't want to come to her that evening. He probably went out into town, either for a deal or to find some relief for his tension. Darcy didn't care a fig about his intentions. She only needed him to leave.

The woman went back to the window and looked out. Her eyes swept the border of the forest again. Darcy had already decided to escape, but she had been waiting for the right moment to run away and slip from under Driscoll's thumb.

Initially, Darcy had come as a guest in Emmett Driscoll's house. However, the woman had been held a prisoner in that bedroom since yesterday. She had come back from her shopping trip earlier than everyone expected her and unwillingly witnessed something she shouldn't have.

Now the expensively furnished room felt like a cage. The walls suffocated Darcy, and the golden decorations danced before her eyes.

The woman rubbed her red-rimmed eyes with the back of her fingers and winced. Her eyes stung, and a pang of pain shot through her puffy eyelids. Tears had dulled the cobalt of her irises, but the dark blue still set off the paleness of her skin.

"Jim, Gabe, and Jon, you and your teams will come with me. Frank and Matthew will hold the fort with their men," Emmett Driscoll's voice shouted distinctly from the front of the house.

Darcy's heart beat faster in anticipation. If Emmett Driscoll's left, she could fly the coop right then. The sun was already setting in the west, and Darcy didn't know the mountain. However, she knew that the night would conceal her movements.

"What about the woman, boss?" a grave tone of voice asked.

Darcy held her breath. She feared Emmett's answer.

'What if he puts a guard under the balcony and one before the bedroom door?' she wondered frantically.

"She won't pose a problem, Gabe. I took care of that," Emmett Driscoll replied to his employee.

PULLED IN

Sarcasm filled the man's voice, and Darcy fairly growled with impotent rage. Her belly revolted with repulsion. Darcy remembered how Emmett had taken care of her with his fists. He had also kicked her a few times for good measure. Worse, the man had laid his hands on her body. In spite of her constant refusals and begging, Driscoll had raped her a couple of times.

Remembering everything, Darcy felt like throwing up again. But then, her stomach was empty. She didn't swallow any food since the beginning of the previous evening. Darcy would only gulp some water now and then when her lips got dry, and her tongue stuck to the roof of her mouth. The mere sight of food made her sick.

Darcy shook her head to get rid of those thoughts. She had more urgent things to do and couldn't wallow in self-pity.

The sound of wheels running over the pebbles in the yard reached her ears. Darcy rubbed her arms with anxiety.

Her eyes searched the patch of woods visible through the balcony doors again. The woman felt her heart in her boots, but she knew what she had to do.

Darcy wiped off her forehead with the back of her hand. The air inside the bedroom was moist and hot, although the ceiling fan was busy. The blades continuously stirred the air coming through the French doors, thrown wide open toward the garden and the forest.

The hypnotic movement of the pallets compelled Darcy's eyelids to drop. Yet, she couldn't fall asleep. She needed to leave right then.

Darcy had made the math. Her only way to freedom was to cross the forest and climb up the mountain slope. She had caught a glimpse of the ridge while driving up toward Emmett's ranch. The sight had intimidated her then. Now she just pushed that thought aside.

Darcy had noticed that Emmett left only a few guards behind when he left the house. About fourteen people milled around, and most of them kept their eyes on the stables.

Emmett feared that someone would snatch his award-winning horses. He didn't believe that someone would dare to breach into his house. So Darcy planned to sneak out the opposite way.

Absently, Darcy wiped her clammy palms off the towel discarded on the back of the chair set before the vanity table. She had taken quite a few showers within the last twenty-four hours to get rid of Emmett's smell. It still clung to her skin and invaded her nostrils, although Emmett hadn't come to her room since the day before.

When she replaced the towel, Darcy avoided looking at her reflection in the mirror. Her face was ashen, and lines had found their way on her forehead. Bruises marred her once beautiful face and smooth arms – a constant reminder of her credulity.

Darcy strode quickly to the bed where she had prepared a pair of blue jeans and a t-shirt earlier. She pulled them on with hurried gestures.

The woman chose to wear sneakers for her hike, and she tied the laces tight. Darcy had never climbed up a mountain, but she didn't think that she could make it in regular shoes.

PULLED IN

Darcy looked around, her mind searching for what else she should take with her.

'*You should have thought of that earlier, girl,*' the woman scolded herself with irritation.

Darcy felt like slapping herself. She wasted precious time on small things.

In the spur of the moment, Darcy fished her ID and a few banknotes from her purse. She left the credit card behind. Films showed that people's moves could be traced if they used credit cards.

After she shoved everything into her pockets, Darcy started toward the balcony doors with purposeful steps. The woman looked over the edge of the suspended terrace.

Darcy had to climb down the trellis, which ran on the side of the balcony, but she could do it. She had climbed a few trees in her adolescence.

Darcy clambered over the brink of the balcony. Men's laughter from the other side of the house reached her ears.

CHAPTER TWO

MOST OF THE TREK, DARCY avoided the slope of the mountain covered with thick bushes and grass. Anyone could have spotted her there. She chose to lose her trail through the patches of dense trees.

Darcy slid on the wet soil and went down hard. However, she braced herself on her knees and hands this time. The fall took the wind out of her, and she groaned.

That wasn't her first fall, though. Luckily, it wasn't the worst, either. The leaves littering the forest floor had protected her. The woman even patted them with affection, although some doubts concerning her sanity lurked in the corner of her mind.

Darcy knew that her skin must have been blue and black by now, on top of the bruises which already covered her body before she left Emmett's grounds.

'It doesn't really matter,' Darcy mumbled to herself when she caught her breath. 'I am free, and that's more important.'

Earlier, am owl had hooted and startled her. Darcy had stepped onto a patch of musty soil and fallen with a thump. She skidded a few yards down the slope.

That fall had scared her out of her mind. The woman had barely broken her fall, and that by pure chance. At the last moment, her fingers had blindly grabbed the trunk of a young tree. God only knew how far the foot of the hill was, and Darcy could live just fine without finding out.

Darcy shook her head to clear it. Exhaustion had caught up with her, and she pushed herself to put a foot in front of the other.

Darcy hadn't slept much the night before, and she had paced across the bedroom most of the day. That had sucked up some of her energy.

Darcy had sneaked out of Emmett's ranch through the back gardens so that the guards wouldn't see her. Then she had hiked through the forest and up the mountain, walking most of the night because of sheer will.

She had dallied only a few minutes here and there to rest and take her bearings. She didn't doubt that she had even walked in circles a few times.

Darcy had moved fast at the beginning of her journey, afraid that Emmett Driscoll's guards would discover her absence and come after her.

Her vivid imagination had created all sorts of scenarios. The woman had even crossed a stream a few times, in case Emmett's goons had brought dogs with them to catch her scent. After a few crossings, she had decided to walk through the stream up on the mountain. She had reasoned that the dogs would lose her track in the water for good.

PULLED IN

When she arrived at Driscoll's ranch, the man had shown her around, pointing to most of the buildings close to the ranch house. Darcy had noticed Emmett Driscoll's pen full of hunting dogs, situated on one side of the ranch yard.

Darcy had also caught snippets of conversations here and there. She understood that they used dogs for hunting. It wasn't apparent what kind of hunt, though. However, she wouldn't put it beyond Emmett to chase after her with the dogs.

After the first few hours of freedom, Darcy had slowed down. Her feet hurt, and she became more concerned about the wildlife on the mountain. She had read about bears and bobcats and didn't plan to be their dinner. A couple of times, Darcy had seen something like red eyes shining in the dark through the leaves. That had scared the wits out of her. She had run like chased by the hounds of hell.

'I will have to find a place to stop and rest,' Darcy thought. 'It will be dawn soon. I can't walk in the daylight anyway. Anybody would spot me easily.'

Darcy feared that even if Emmett's people wouldn't see her, someone else might, and they would tell on her.

The woman pushed herself off the ground with determination and grimaced when a sharp pain crossed her right knee. 'Damn, not an easy thing to wander through the forest at night,' Darcy reflected with acrimony, rubbing her knee. 'Especially after it rained,' she mumbled under her breath.

Another sharp pain made her swore, and Darcy didn't abstain but uttered all the bad words she had learned during her last stint at a ranch near Missoula. There wasn't anyone nearby to hear her swearing, after all.

It had rained furiously for about a couple of hours earlier. It had soaked Darcy to the skin, and the water had saturated the soil. The woman thought that it poured too much, and the ground couldn't absorb all the water. Nonetheless, she continued dragging her feet through the slime on the ground.

Now and then, a gust of wind swirled in the air, and the young woman shivered. But then, Darcy didn't feel the nippy bite of the night air. The effort had heated her, and she had been sweating profusely.

Suddenly, the forest made way to shrubs and grass. A pale moon shone over Darcy's head, so the woman had a better view of her surroundings.

Her eyes swept over the slanted terrain, and she noticed the menacing sharp rocks erected in the distance. Darcy resolved to stride toward them and find a cave or something where she could lay down over the day, although she didn't have a precise idea in her head.

Darcy headed up, following an oblique trajectory. The woman didn't dare to brave the steep incline directly. Her strenuous walk had depleted her stamina, and the side of the mountain tilted at about forty-five degrees.

Darcy tripped over a thick root, and once more, she kissed the ground with a loud woof. When she caught her breath, she swore again.

Darcy thought of lingering on the ground for a while but changed her mind fast. She stood up, using the trunk of a tree for support. Once on her feet, she breathed deeply and allowed herself a moment of rest.

PULLED IN

The woman leaned on a tree trunk with a sigh of relief. Then annoyed, she glanced down at her dirty pants and sneakers. A thick coat of filth covered nearly every inch of her body.

Darcy scowled with disgust, but then she thought better. She reflected that being covered with mud was better than having Emmett on top of her, which disgusted her. Anything was better than that.

Nevertheless, after a moment of reflection, she reconsidered. She wouldn't have liked it if a bear had eaten her. Nothing else bothered her.

Darcy shrugged and decided to continue her journey. She pushed ahead, but her legs shook already, and the woman knew that she needed to stop soon.

Nevertheless, after a moment of reflection, she reconsidered. She wouldn't have liked it if a bear had eaten her. Nothing else bothered her.

Darcy shrugged and decided to continue her journey. She pushed ahead, but her legs shook already, and the woman knew that she needed to stop soon.

CHAPTER THREE

DARCY WOKE UP WITH a startle, rubbed her eyes, and yawned. The woman scrambled for a few seconds and then sat up with a groan. Her muscles protested loudly. The enclosure of rocks created a narrow chamber, and Darcy had slept in an awkward position, with her knees gathered to her chest.

Darcy tried to accustom her eyes to the dark, and only then she realized that something had interrupted her sleep, so she decided to go out and see what happened.

Darcy began crawling toward the mouth of the cave. She already knew that side of the cave as well as the back of her hand. She had crossed it several times by then.

The water had dug the narrow passage in the rocks along the time. There wasn't too much room to move, and it narrowed even more in some places, so Darcy scratched her elbows, arms, and knees, but she persevered doggedly.

Darcy had stumbled onto the opening of the passage at dawn and crawled for over fifty paces before the makeshift cave widened enough so that she could lie down in a fetus position. She had fallen asleep like a log.

Darcy wriggled through the passage and reached the exterior wall of the cave only after a few minutes this time. She had acquired enough practice. Her muscles screamed, but she clenched her teeth and endured.

When she reached the exterior mouth of the tunnel, Darcy glanced at the sky. She realized that she had virtually slept all morning and a good part of the afternoon. Various noises had woken her up several times during the night, and Darcy had crawled back outside every time to see what was going on. She was worried that Emmett had found her.

Now that she reached the mouth of the cave, the noise that had disturbed Darcy's sleep became distinctive. Hooves eating the ground sounded closer to her location, and their thunder pounded louder in her ears.

Darcy glued herself to the rocky floor. The opening wasn't broad enough, and Darcy's line of vision was abysmal, but she could listen at least.

"Where the heck is that cursed woman?" a rusty voice inquired with irritation.

Darcy recognized the timbre of that voice, and her heart stopped for a moment. She couldn't put a name on it, but it was clear that Emmett's men had found her.

"You should know," another man's voice answered with obvious irony. "You were supposed to take care of the woman if I remember correctly."

A string of crude curses followed, and Darcy cringed, but she kept quiet. That man's irritation didn't promise anything good for her if they found her, and she prayed that he didn't discover her position.

PULLED IN

"Where the hell did she go?" the first voice asked with bewilderment. "We've looked practically everywhere."

"Are you asking me, Frank?" the second man replied. "Maybe she got eaten by a bobcat or a bear," the man advanced the idea in a hopeful tone of voice.

"We'd have seen a trace or something," Frank countered in a frustrated tone of voice.

"With that rain last night, traces might have disappeared," a third voice intervened.

Darcy noticed with amazement that the voice belonged to a very young man. She didn't think the boy was even twenty.

"Shut your mouth, kiddo," Frank barked. "We'd have seen the traces of her steps in the mud," he retorted.

"Not really," another man said, and now, Darcy recognized Gabe's voice.

She wouldn't forget Gabe. The man had forbidden Darcy to go out in the garden the previous day.

Gabe's eyes betrayed the man's brutishness. He even had the mug of a thug, and his slanted black eyes had looked at her as if she were a bug he wanted to squash under his foot. The man's blatant disregard for another human being scared her witless.

"It depends on how much it rained after she had passed along the trail," Gabe drawled. "And if she got to this rocky area, there's no way we can find out where she went from here. We shouldn't have sent the dogs back to the ranch, even if they'd lost her trail at the stream," he observed in a hard tone of voice now, and his words betrayed a mute reproach for his mate.

Frank swore again, apparently in agreement with Gabe's last assessment. Frank's voice showed that what Emmett would do if they didn't find Darcy terrified the man.

The woman didn't intend to make their job easier, so she didn't move a muscle, afraid that she would give her position away. The men had chosen their master, and she didn't care about what happened to them. In her opinion, they deserved everything that came their way.

"It's already after four," the younger man said. "I think we should grab something to eat and continue our search later. I haven't swallowed anything since morning," the boy complained.

"I don't see why we have to starve," he pointed out.

"We don't have time to eat, boy," Frank's voice whipped the young man.

"Why not?" Gabe intervened. "It's not like we'd waste too much time if we stopped and had a bite. I suppose you've brought something with you, Dean?" he inquired.

Darcy's heart froze. She was famished and couldn't bear the thought that they would eat right there, nearby to her hide-out. Besides, she didn't know how long she could hold the same position.

"I haven't thought of taking any food with me," the young man admitted.

Gabe looked around at the men and noticed that all of them shook their heads.

"Good thinking, people," Gabe observed with irony. "We'll have to catch a cottontail. We'll make a fire and roast it," he concluded.

PULLED IN

"We don't have time for that," Frank snapped. "God knows where the woman has gone by now, and I don't want to lose my head for a light skirt," the man snarled and then spat with disgust.

"No one will take your head if we stop for a bite, Frank" Gabe waved his comrade's worries aside with indifference.

"The men won't say a thing about our break to Driscoll, will you?" he turned to the rest of their party and pierced them with a black gaze. "Keep in mind that you'll also get into trouble if he hears that we stopped our hunt to eat," Gabe warned them in a sharp tone of voice.

Darcy noticed that two of them seemed to hesitate for a few seconds, but then they nodded.

"So then we're on the same page here," Gabe concluded. "Let's find ourselves a cottontail or two," he signaled them to follow him. "Two or maybe even three would be better. We won't fill our bellies with only one," the man threw the words over his shoulder with ugly laughter.

Then he galloped down the slope toward the grasslands, and the men followed him. The clatter of hooves filled the air, and Darcy held her breath, full of hope.

Darcy kept her position at the edge of the cave for a while. She didn't dare to move from there until the men had departed and left the area.

She listened hard until she couldn't hear their voices or the gallop of the horses anymore. Then she ventured to look around from behind the surrounding rocks.

Darcy noticed that the sun had already reached the west side of the sky. However, there wasn't anyone nearby, and she sighed with relief.

For a moment or two, she had feared that the men played with her, misleading and letting her believe that she was safe.

Darcy also thanked the heavens that the men hadn't decided to build that fire there and cook their meat. She was famished and wouldn't have borne the smell of freshly fried roast. Her stomach was growling only at the thought of food.

The woman crawled out of the so-called cave. Once she got out in the open, Darcy stretched in spite of all the aches tormenting her body. She massaged her calves energetically to restore blood circulation in her limbs and felt tickles everywhere.

Somewhat recovered, Darcy decided to go around the group of rocks covering the cave and reach the other side of the hill. She had her lips cracked, and her throat parched, so she hoped to find some water along the way.

The woman started up the hill again, clinging to bushes and grass in places where the ascent proved difficult. She began to pant in no time at all, and her t-shirt stuck to her back. A coat of perspiration glowed on her face and chest. Blisters already covered her feet in the aftermath of the previous night's hike, and every step was pure torture.

Darcy glanced up at the solitary peaks braving the sky and understood that the ascent wouldn't be easy. However, the woman locked her teeth and continued climbing.

An eagle shot through the skies, gliding graciously above the butte. It disappeared beyond the rocky tops, and Darcy envied the bird and its smooth journey.

The woman's stomach growled, and she tried to move her thoughts away from food. What she needed most was water.

CHAPTER FOUR

NICK COULDN'T SEE AT two feet before his eyes. He looked up and noticed that a gray blanket of clouds covered the night sky. The man thought that the moon must be hiding behind the clouds, and with dismay, he cursed the cold, humid fog that surrounded everything.

The night's atmosphere matched his mood. The man felt restless, and something bothered him, although he didn't know precisely what.

The humid air had left wet traces on his exposed skin, and even though it was cold, Nick still had to wipe his brow. Then he rubbed his fingers off his denim pants and groaned. Everything annoyed him that night.

Nick couldn't wait to go inside and simmer in his favorite armchair set before the fireplace in the salon. His cottage became cold at that time of the year, even during the day. However, Nick didn't need to light a fire just yet. But then, the man often enjoyed a cozy atmosphere at the end of a day with hard work. When the summer made way to fall, he would always light a small fire in the fireplace.

However, the man couldn't go inside just yet. He had something else to do. Nick had sensed an unusual scent nearby. The smell of gardenia mixed with fresh blood and created a unique combination. Nick had to check and see what it was. He had survived and reached his ripen age of thirty-eight by being cautious, after all.

The smell of flowers didn't bother Nick, although it didn't belong there. However, he worried about the scent of blood. Nick's instincts screamed, telling him about someone's presence at the far end of the ranch yard.

Someone hunched very close to the bushes of white flowers, whose name he had never known. Not that Nick would have cared about their darn species. The plants merely brought some color to the otherwise gray and sparsely green enclosure.

The scent of fresh flowers mingled with something a bit sour, reminding Nick of the sweat lingering on the body after a hard day of work. The smell wasn't as pungent as his in similar circumstances, though.

His ears caught a light breath, and Nick thought of a small animal, lying down and keeping quiet, afraid of the hunter who tracked him. That nauseated Nick.

A flash of a memorable hunting day crossed his mind. He still loathed that day deeply. At the time, he had often found himself a mere puppet in other people's hands, and Nick couldn't stand the lack of control. That day, Nick's uncle had taken him out into the woods for the first time, intending to show to the boy what authentic killing meant.

'It'll make a man out of your pansy-ass,' the overweight thirty-something-old man had said to Nick with a smirk on his face. He enjoyed Nick's fear and horrified curiosity.

'Yeah, you were a real man, uncle. A real killer,' Nick thought and tasted the bitterness of his bile on the tongue.

His uncle's face, with clumped dirty locks, hanging around the sides of the man's face, danced before Nick's eyes. A big man, with meaty hands, his uncle loved inflicting pain without remorse or discrimination.

The old bag of wind enjoyed killing and not only beasts in the woods. He had tried his knife on a few women's bodies as well. Thankfully, the police had locked him down for life, although that had come a bit too late. A few women had already lost their lives under the man's knife.

Nick shook off his thoughts and resolved to come back to more earthy and pressing matters. After all, he still had to find out who was hiding in his bushes in the dark.

Nick never left things to the whims of chance. Life had taught him better than that, and his previous sting in special ops had also seasoned his instincts. The man preferred to know his enemy and strike first, so he headed to the bushes with long strides.

"Hey, you," Nick shouted at the person hiding in the bushes after he stopped at about three feet away, ready for any attack.

Nick's ears pricked, ready to catch the slightest noise. No answer came back, but the intruder's breathing rhythm changed and became shallow and louder.

Fright reverberated in the unconscious sigh that reached Nick's ears a few seconds later. The intruder chocked it immediately, but it was too late. The smell of sweat became stronger, and Nick's nostrils flared.

For a fleeting moment, Nick thought of going back to the house. He could forget about the person hiding in the shrubbery. It didn't look like they would pose a threat to him. It was more likely someone with their own issues.

Nick didn't interfere in other people's troubles. That line of action had worked just fine for him until then. After all, Nick wasn't the man to offer comfort, or hope, or what the hell people might have expected from the others.

Nick had resolved to turn around and go back to the house when another stifled sigh reached him. He turned his head back to the bushes with resignation.

Almost unwillingly, stepping onto his heart and cursing himself ten times for being a fool, Nick shook his head. The urge to help that poor being appeared to be stronger than his indifference.

With a sigh of his own, Nick walked toward the bushes with massive steps. He made noise on purpose to warn the person lying down in the undergrowth that he was coming so that they wouldn't be taken by surprise.

Nick said in a loud tone of voice, "I'm coming to you. Come out of the bushes so that I could see who you are!"

The rustiness of his voice didn't seem to reassure much the person hunched in the shrubberies, and once more, no answer came from the scrubs. Now no breathing reached Nick's ears, either, and the man suspected that the person held their breath, most likely because of fear.

"Don't be afraid," Nick shouted again. "I'm not going to take a piece out of you, but you have to come out of there. I need to see who I am dealing with," he explained patiently in a measured tone of voice.

PULLED IN

No one replied, and Nick cursed viciously. He decided to get closer to the shrubs. Now the breath had become shallower, a sign that the person's fear had turned into terror.

Nick knew he was a big man. Many had resembled him to a bear and looked at him with apprehension when he was in attack mode. However, the last time he had looked at himself in the mirror while trimming his stubble, Nick hadn't seen anything very threatening in his appearance. Of course, if he discounted the scar which marred his left cheek – a sign of his previous life when he was able to handle a knife better than anything else.

Nonetheless, Nick didn't think that anyone would notice the scar in the dark if they didn't have catlike vision. The light from the porch didn't reach so far out, and shadows abounded there.

With giant strides, Nick reached the bushes and distinguished a shadow clinched on the ground.

"What are you doing there?" Nick asked in a softer tone of voice.

In spite of his efforts, his inquiry remained without reply. However, it wasn't as if Nick didn't expect that.

The man sensed that the person was staring at him. With a resigned shake of his head, Nick reached out to help the shadow stand up. The tiny human package turned into a wildcat in a second and started fighting him with a warrior-like cry.

A small, cold fist punched Nick in the chin. The stretched fingers of the attacker's other hand aimed at the side of Nick's face. At least one nail scratched his skin through the stubble, and a distinct hiss sounded in Nick's ears.

Confronted with a fierce attack, Nick lost his patience. Nick snarled, and his fingers encircled the upper limbs of his opponent tightly, pulling the person toward him in the process. The arms he had grabbed felt rounded but frail under his fingers, and Nick assumed that he was holding either a child or a woman. The man forced himself to restrain his anger and strength at once. He had never fought against a child or a woman and didn't intend to start doing it right then.

Nonetheless, he half-dragged and half-carried the small package toward the porch of the house where a lamp hung from the ceiling. Nick had to make some effort to reach the porch with his little burden. The person wriggled in his arms, and a few times, Nick almost dropped them.

When he got under the light on the porch, Nick discovered that he was holding a young woman, and she didn't look well at all. The woman's clothes were torn and dirty. He assumed that she had trampled through the woods and over a roughened land.

The imprint of a hammy fist marred the right side of the woman's face, and an angry bruise tainted the corner of her mouth. Her nose had bled, and a trail of clotted blood had smeared her upper lip and chin. The woman had probably tried to wipe the blood off several times, and Nick noticed the result of her efforts.

In Nick's opinion, the woman wasn't even thirty yet. Fear shone wildly in her cobalt eyes and dilated her glassy pupils. In spite of her fright, her furrowed brows betrayed her deep anger.

Nick's dark brown eyes searched her face. He understood that she was determined to fight him back by any means necessary, and regardless of the outcome.

That almost brought a smile to Nick's lips. Unless the woman had been an indisputable martial arts expert, she wouldn't have stood a chance against him. He freed the woman's arms with slow gestures and opened the door to the cottage.

"You may get inside," he said mildly, and with an almost elegant wave of his fingers, he invited her to step into his house.

His tone didn't sound menacing, but the woman cringed at his words, and her lips quivered. In spite of those outward signs of fear, Nick sensed that the woman was more than ready to dig her nails into his jugular, and he shook his head. A shadow of a smile appearing briefly on his lips.

However, at a closer look, the woman looked tired and depleted. Her deep paleness worried him, and now the man shook his head in dismay.

"Don't worry," Nick told her, and bitterness sounded in his voice. "I don't attack defenseless women. At least, not in this lifetime, sweetheart," he added in a dry voice.

Nick infused a particular bite into his words. He imagined that sarcasm might bring some color to the woman's face, and he wasn't wrong. The woman's frown deepened, and a faint blush spread over her skin. Nick read on her features that she didn't believe his words, and probably she had reasons to be cautious.

The young woman took a step back to put some distance between them, and she nearly fell down the stairs. With another sigh filled with dismay, Nick reached out and grabbed her arm again to stop her from sprawling down the stairs. Then he spoke once more, and now irritation rang in his voice. "Don't be stupid, woman! It's too late at night for that. It's damn too dark now, and the air will turn cold soon. You shouldn't wander outside on the mountain on your own. I promise you that I'm not going to touch you, and I always keep my word. It's not like you look desirable right now, anyway. I will only try to keep you warm and out of trouble for one night if that's possible, of course. With your behavior, you do ask for a good spanking," Nick added in a harsh tone of voice, his patience practically gone out of the window.

That night didn't turn out as he had expected. The man had hoped to spend a quiet night in the solitude of his cottage. Now he was saddled with an unwanted guest.

Tears welled into the woman's eyes, and the man's right brow climbed up his forehead. Nick wondered if relief made her crying, but he doubted that. It was more likely that his last words had brought the tears into her eyes. Once more, he sighed in dismay.

The woman still stared at him as if she couldn't trust him. But then, at least, she didn't step back again and didn't try to shake off his hand either. She seemed to have chosen a different way of action.

'Maybe she's thinking to stare me into submission,' Nick reflected maliciously.

Nick waved toward the door once more, and the woman accepted the invitation. She entered the cottage without a word. It looked like she had decided to wait and see what the man was going to do next.

Nick imagined that the best thing he could do was to reassure her that he didn't have any evil intentions toward her. The man let her go ahead and closed the door behind them.

Then, he walked around the woman, careful not to touch her and show her the way to the first room of the cottage, which played the role of a living room and a dining-room at the same time.

Darcy looked warily around, and her pulse slowed down. She didn't know why, but when her eyes swept around the room full of mismatched pieces of furniture, she felt better. The eclectic style warmed the place, even though that salon seemed far too manly for her taste.

At the other end of the room, Darcy spotted an anemic fire dancing in the fireplace. After she had been in the cold and humidity outside for so long, she perked up.

The tongues of the flames touched the grill set before the fire and brought Darcy a measure of comfort and reassurance.

The young woman's mood improved, but still, Darcy didn't feel at ease. She kept her guard up and watched the man's every move from under her lashes.

Darcy maintained a reasonable distance between the two of them. She had already felt the man's strength and knew that she couldn't fight him back if she had to.

Nick watched her as well and noticed that the woman didn't trust him. The man didn't mind her caution. He understood that she had her reasons. They were written all over her body, after all.

Someone had done bad things to that slip of a woman, and Nick knew that she wouldn't forget any of what had happened to her soon.

Nick sighed and shook his head. He flexed his shoulders and waved at her again, directing her to an armchair close to the fireplace.

Nick schooled his features so that his face didn't betray any of his pity. The man didn't know how the woman would take it, and he wasn't in any mood to find out. He watched her as she moseyed carefully toward the fireplace. Darcy kept him in sight all the time, ready to bolt if he had come closer.

Her moves reminded Nick of a small wild animal, with hunters on her trail. Yet, she seemed willing to do her utmost to survive, and he respected that. Not everyone had survival skills or the strength to apply them.

Her appearance aroused Nick's curiosity. He would have liked to find out what had happened to her, yet he wasn't interested enough to ask. Anyway, the man doubted that he would have wanted to hear her answer.

During his lifetime, Nick had witnessed a lot of things. He had first-hand knowledge about what kind of bad things a human being was capable of inflicting on another.

Nick's eyes assessed the woman once more. She needed a bath to clean up the dirt of her journey out of hell. Nick shook his head in dismay. He would have enjoyed laying his hands on whoever had left those marks on the woman's face. The bastard needed to get a taste of his own medicine. Nick despised cowards, who abused the weaker.

"I'm going to make something warm for you to drink and eat," he said quietly.

Darcy winced as if she didn't think that he would talk. Nick's words surprised her because she hadn't expected any thoughtful gesture from him.

"Meanwhile, if you want, of course, because no one is pushing you from behind, there's a bathroom upstairs, the third door on the right," Nick continued.

PULLED IN

He noticed that the woman's eyes widened in surprise and thought to reassure her.

"The bathroom has got a good lock on the door, so you should feel safe enough. You will find everything you need there. You need a little refreshing, don't you think?" Nick tried to persuade her in a soft tone of voice.

The woman didn't answer him. Nick waited for a few seconds, but then he gave up.

Either the woman wasn't able to speak, or she had decided not to talk with another man in her lifetime. That wouldn't have surprised him.

Nick didn't care about her reasons, though. He just headed to the kitchen and stopped paying any outward attention to her. He imagined that she might feel more at ease that way.

The woman's tired eyes followed Nick's movements attentively. Only when she was sure that the man wouldn't come back, Darcy turned around and headed upstairs. She tried to walk as noiselessly as possible and kept glancing back in Nick's direction all the time.

Darcy did need to get rid of all the dirt, which covered her body in a thick layer. Nonetheless, she was afraid that everything was just a ruse, and the man toyed with her.

Nick did return with quiet steps, just in time to see the young woman disappearing on the landing. However, he didn't leave the kitchen but stopped in the doorway.

A bitter grin slowly flourished on his lips. The woman's way of doing things amused him. Nevertheless, it also saddened him to see her so apprehensive about everything. Nick shook his head, and with a shrug, he strode back into the kitchen. Once in there, he put a pot on the stove with the thought of making her some hot tea.

Nick knew that the humidity and the cold of the night must have seeped into her bones, and he thought that she would welcome something warm and soothing.

Finishing with that, Nick decided to warm the leftovers of the stew he had cooked for himself that afternoon. The dish would have lasted for two or three days if he had been alone. Nick loathed cooking, and therefore he prepared everything in large batches for a few days. It meant less time spent in the kitchen.

Nick stirred the food into the pot, and an eyebrow climbed up his forehead. He grimaced while watching the concoction with suspicion.

The man knew the limitations of his cooking skills. He had tasted his stew that evening and added a lot of pepper to smother the taste. Now he wondered how the woman would welcome his food.

Nick's attempts in the kitchen had never been very successful. He either burnt the food or undercooked it. Sometimes, the food turned out utterly tasteless, and that was a real bother. Nick, at his core, was a gourmand. Nick's cooking hadn't improved too much over time, although he had made some progress over the last few years.

In about ten minutes, Nick finished with everything and waited for the woman to return to the dining room. He had already finished setting everything on one end of the table and decided to sit in a chair at the other end. He had imagined that the woman would like some distance between the two of them.

PULLED IN

Nick had reflected upon what might have happened to his guest to push her to brave the mountain. He despised men who hurt women. In general, men's physical built made it easier for them to prey on a female and inflict painful punishments. Nick had met a few individuals not endowed enough for that, but not many.

Nick's make up was different. If a woman upset him, he just left. He didn't see any sense in hitting or raping a woman or, God knows, what might have happened to his peculiar guest.

Nick was shaking his head in dismay once more when his uninvited visitor climbed down the stairs with hesitant steps. The woman had kept the mudded jeans, but now she wore one of Nick's white t-shirts. He left a stack of them in the bathroom that afternoon after he had washed and folded them.

The soft cotton hugged her curves, and Nick raised his left brow in surprise but refrained from saying anything. His chocolate eyes just zeroed in appreciatively on a few choice spots on the woman's curvy body for a few seconds. Then he looked up straight into her eyes so that she didn't get any wrong ideas.

Nick wouldn't have thought her courageous enough to take something from him, or at least not without asking.

'One point for her,' he reflected. 'You were wrong, man, and you know well that you can't afford to be wrong. Be careful! She's got some spine, you know?'

Nick also noticed that the woman had washed her ebony hair, and now it fell on her shoulders in an ink-like luscious mass. She hadn't bothered to dry it properly.

The traces of blood, which spotted her face earlier, had also vanished, and her cobalt eyes lit her pale skin. However, bruises still marked her face and arms and made her look more vulnerable than Nick would have liked her to be. Faced with a woman in need, the man showed particular weakness, and he minded that. Nick had never been at ease with vulnerable women and always preferred the feisty ones, who would take his eyes out rather than showing any vulnerability in front of him.

But then, Nick would have preferred not to have any woman in his vicinity right that moment. Somewhat hollow, he didn't feel like putting up with a woman's intricate mind.

Nick pushed his disturbing thoughts aside with a shrug. Silently, he waved his fingers toward the plate and cup, he had set on the table for her earlier, and wordlessly, he invited her to have dinner.

Darcy sat down in the assigned chair with timidity. However, the woman didn't dare to take her wary eyes off him. After what she had gone through that damn day and the previous hellish days, she couldn't trust that man or any other, for that matter. In a brief period, she had learned that men were sleek and bent to take whatever they wanted. They didn't feel any remorse for their actions if that suited them.

Darcy knew that she wasn't equipped or trained to protect herself, and the man sitting at the table opposite her was tall and broad. He was built like a bear.

She couldn't discern anything smooth or sweet inside him. He was rough and hard all over. The long, ragged scar on his face was like a screaming label.

PULLED IN

The woman began eating with rushed gestures. Darcy was starving, and besides, she didn't want to linger in the man's presence for long. While shoveling the tasteless food into her mouth, she kept observing her host from under her lashes. She needed only a few minutes to polish her plate.

Darcy couldn't even remember when she had eaten the last time, but definitely not that day. She had left the cage in the evening the day before and hadn't dared to get closer to the beaten paths.

She hadn't even looked for berries, afraid of bears and other creatures.

After she finished her food and swallowed her tea, Darcy set the cup on the table with measured gestures. Then she intertwined her fingers in her lap and merely waited. The woman couldn't find the strength to speak, and anyway, she had no idea what she could say to Nick.

The man intrigued her, but Darcy didn't believe that she had anything in common with him. He wasn't part of her world, and she had never met a man just like him.

Darcy knew the horse racing world and very little beyond that. Besides that, she felt that the man didn't belong to any world at all.

"Can you tell me your name?" Nick asked her. His tone of voice was hushed so that she didn't find his words threatening.

Darcy didn't answer him immediately. The woman just watched him with her cobalt eyes. They shone full of secrets and disillusionment. The silence stretched for a few more seconds and filled the room with palpable tension.

"We'd work better together if I knew your name. I can't shout at you something like 'Hey, you!' all the time, can I?" Nick insisted, and now some impatience tainted his tone of voice.

The woman winced at first, but then, she tilted her head and considered his words for a few moments. Darcy seemed to ponder the pro and counter-arguments on a long list as if he asked her to explain the big bang theory.

Nick clenched his teeth with frustration and glared at her. After a few long minutes, the woman finally nodded, decided to answer his question.

"Darcy," she replied to him in a strangled tone of voice.

"All right, Darcy," he said, and his voice sounded calmer now. "I'm Nick. Now you can call my name if you need me," he told her. 'Let's hope you won't,' he continued in his mind.

Darcy merely blinked, but she didn't bother to reply. The woman doubted that she would need him. She didn't trust him enough for that.

Nick flexed his fists and narrowed his eyes. The young woman started to get on his nerves with that scared-rabbit behavior. He understood cautiousness but not fear.

"I'm going to give you a room with a lock on the door so that you would feel safe, Darcy. I don't know who did that to you," he added, pointing his chin toward her face. "Anyway, at least tonight, you can find some peace in my cottage. No one will bother you. All right?"

PULLED IN

Darcy searched Nick's face and eyes warily for a few moments. She seemed to take his measure and analyze his words. When she made up her mind, she nodded and replied to him in a hoarse tone of voice, "Okay, I'll trust you as long as I have a key in my hand."

Nick approved of her words, and an ironic grin tugged at the corners of his mouth. He waved toward Darcy to stand up and then headed out of the room and up the stairs in front of her. Usually, Nick was reticent of having an unwanted guest underfoot, but suddenly, he wasn't sorry that he was put in the situation to offer her shelter.

Nick couldn't also refrain from thinking that if he had wanted Darcy badly enough, the locked door wouldn't have stopped him. He could have broken that obstacle down with little effort and in a matter of seconds. He wondered that Darcy hadn't thought of that, considering that she was so frightened and cautious.

The man would have lied to himself if he had said that the woman didn't arouse something inside him. But then, for the moment, Darcy seemed defenseless and lost, and he couldn't try anything, even if he had wanted to charm the panties off her.

Anyway, Nick had recently had his problems with women only a few months before. He didn't need any new troubles right then. The man enjoyed his solitude too much to get involved in a new relationship.

Once they reached the upper floor, Nick put a key in Darcy's shaky hand. He showed her to the second door in the hallway. Afterward, with a brief nod and without words, the man turned back and went downstairs again. He left Darcy to watch his departing silhouette with wide eyes.

Darcy couldn't believe her luck. She hadn't hoped to find a safe shelter for the night. It seemed too good to be true, so she went into the room and locked the door. She needed that illusion of security, at least.

At the sound of the key turned into the lock, Nick grinned again, and only then, the man realized with some surprise that he hadn't smiled in months. That thought brought a frown between his thick eyebrows.

CHAPTER FIVE

DARCY DIDN'T TAKE OFF the t-shirt she had *borrowed* from Nick earlier. She discarded only her dirty jeans and sneakers. Then she stretched carefully on the bed, afraid that she would jar something inside her body and closed her eyes.

The bed appeared to be a relic forgotten in that cottage sometime at the end of the eighteenth century.

The piece of furniture was quaint, but it hadn't been an easy feat for Darcy to climb onto the straw mattress, which reached up to her hip. The woman's muscles screamed at every move anyway, and getting onto the bed had worsened her aches.

Darcy's entire body hurt because of the fists or boots that had made contact with her skin and bones or the tumbles taken during the crazy race through the forest and upward the slope of the mountain.

The ache in her cheek was the worst, and Darcy touched the injured cheekbone gingerly, thinking that she should have put something cold on it to soothe the abused skin.

However, Darcy didn't dare to ask anything else from the man downstairs. Nick had already given her more than she expected when he dragged her onto his porch.

Darcy sighed silently and tried to move her thoughts on to something else, willing her aches to go away. Whenever she found herself in the wrong place, she would retreat in the memories of the days when her father was still alive.

Darcy was a single child. Their little family moved around a lot because of her father's profession. But then, Darcy had never resented him because of that. Those years represented her golden years.

Once her father passed away, her life had changed dramatically. Darcy didn't need all her fingers to count the good days she had known afterward. Darcy shook her head in sadness and resolved to find solace in her recollections once more.

The woman had barely closed her eyes when a knock at the door startled her. Fear grabbed Darcy by the throat with steely fingers, and she gasped for air. Darcy cursed herself for her naivety. She had believed that she found a safe haven, and now she would pay for her stupidity.

"Darcy, it's me," Nick said in a quiet tone of voice from behind the door. "I've just remembered that you needed something for the bruise on your face. I've brought you a piece of frozen meat," he explained his presence at her door, and his tone of voice tried to appease her fear. "Just half-open the door, and stretch your hand," he suggested.

Nick knew that his coming back to her door in the middle of the night would frighten the young woman. After stating his intentions, the man waited patiently for Darcy to make up her mind. Nick decided not to insist if she preferred to remain behind the locked door.

PULLED IN

Darcy climbed down the bed with difficulty and tiptoed to the door cautiously. Her legs shook, and she had broken into a cold sweat, which froze her skin under the t-shirt.

The woman tried twice to unlock the door. Her fingers quivered, and she couldn't make them work. Darcy opened the door just a crack. Her fingers reached out and snatched the piece of meat from Nick's hand with a brusque gesture.

"Thank you," Darcy mumbled quickly and shut the door in the man's face.

She turned the key in the lock again swiftly. Her fingers listened to her now, and Darcy made sure that the door was safely locked. Afterward, she sighed with relief. Now she had her space back, although she couldn't be sure that the man would leave her alone for the remaining of the night.

Nick smiled with bitter irony from behind the closed door. He imagined that Darcy must have been scared out of her mind to react that way. The man shook his head as if he couldn't believe that things like that could happen.

But then, he knew better. Such things happened all the time. Sometimes, people went through worse things than that. Only a few people enjoyed a peaceful and happy life. Nick hadn't been one of them, and the young woman behind the locked door didn't seem to be one of those either.

Nick returned downstairs once more and put out all the lights, except the lamp on the porch. He remained outside for about half an hour to smoke and ponder upon the twists that life relentlessly threw at him.

That seemed to be one of those very few nights when Nick felt lonely and deserted. Usually, he thought that he didn't need anyone else in his life.

Nick wondered in passing if he was lying to himself but avoided answering his own question. He doubted that he would have liked the answer.

Nick listened to the quietness of the night. Suddenly, the shrieks of an owl in the distance shredded the silence. The man shook his head to clear it and put out his cigarette. He went back into the cottage, locked the front door, and decided to go to bed. He would wake up before dawn in the morning, and daybreak drew near. His horses would expect that Nick did his job. They wouldn't care whether he slept enough or not.

Darcy's sobs reached the man's ears when he passed by her door, and Nick shrugged with impotence. He couldn't do anything for her, so he didn't break his stride toward his room. If he had tried to offer her comfort, Darcy would have fought him back, and he didn't feel like facing her rejection right then.

After a quick shower, Nick lay in his bed awake for a long time, listening to the familiar noises of the night and the woman's bitter cry. Darcy's pain wormed its way into his heart, and that surprised him. Nick would have thought that his heart had turned to stone during the last two or even three decades. When Darcy's cry stopped, Nick finally fell asleep.

CHAPTER SIX

THE LIGHT OF THE DAY teased her eyelashes, and Darcy woke up dizzy and confused. She didn't know where she was. Fear, her omnipresent and faithful companion, joined her again. The woman grabbed the edge of the blanket with shaky fingers.

She looked around, searching for enemies. Her widened eyes tried to identify anything that she could use as a weapon.

Darcy still shook when everything came back to her. She remembered where she was and how she got there.

The young woman couldn't explain why, but peace filled her when Nick's image popped into her mind. However, Darcy knew that she shouldn't relax in his presence. She didn't know the slightest thing about her bear of a host or what she could expect from him.

Darcy didn't know what to think about the man. She had never met someone remotely close to him. Nonetheless, Nick had offered her shelter when she was in dire need of a place to put her head down, and Darcy was grateful to him for that.

And yet, she could read unfathomable knowledge in his coffee eyes whenever he trained his pupils on her. That man had seen much more of the world than she had. She couldn't even begin to understand what went through his mind when that bitter grin tugged at the corners of his mouth.

Besides that, Darcy couldn't trust anyone, even though the giant seemed to be a good man. Her recent bad experiences made Darcy wary. She couldn't risk her heart or life anymore. She had learned that she couldn't trust her instincts when it came to men.

Noises came from downstairs, and Darcy imagined that her strange host had also woken up. She had no idea what he was doing on the main floor, and curiosity made her itchy to go there too.

The woman threw the blanket away, ready to climb out of bed. Her fingers touched a wet spot, and she shuddered. Darcy looked down and spotted the piece of frozen meat, which Nick had brought to her last night. It had fallen on the sheet and defrosted. Annoyed, Darcy grimaced and picked it up to take it downstairs with her.

First, Darcy half-opened the door and peeked outside. No one was in sight, so Darcy strode to the bathroom with quick steps.

Her heart drummed in her chest, and her legs shook. Once she got inside the room, Darcy locked the door with a sigh of relief. She threw the meat in the sink and leaned against the white porcelain bowl.

PULLED IN

The young woman had slept for almost six hours, but tiredness still languished in her bones. She felt sluggish, and her muscles cramped. Her bruises bothered her more now than when she went to bed the night before.

After she wallowed in self-pity for a few moments, Darcy washed her face and neck with brisk gestures. Her eyes darted to the shower stall longingly, but she didn't find the strength to get inside and take a shower.

Darcy looked at herself in the mirror and grimaced when her eyes fell on the bruises on her face. She didn't look good at all, and she had thought that the look of her face would improve somehow until the next day. She had been wrong.

The side of her face hadn't swollen very much thanks to the cold meat Nick gave to her. She had fallen asleep while holding it on her cheekbone, but it still had done the trick.

Darcy closed her eyes for a few moments again and breathed deeply. Then she grabbed the homespun towel hanging on the towel-holder and dried her face.

With a last look at her reflection in the mirror, the young woman decided to stop hiding and go downstairs. She needed to see what her host was doing there.

When she reached the kitchen, Darcy's eyes lay directly on Nick. He stood in front of the stove, cooking something that smelt really good. Her eyes widened. Darcy had never seen a man preparing food before, not even her father, and Nick's actions bewildered her. Still, pangs of hunger clawed at her belly, and she wondered what Nick was fixing.

Nick had felt Darcy's presence the very moment she stepped at the bottom of the stairs. However, when she came into the kitchen, he didn't turn his head toward her.

Nick didn't want to frighten the woman by betraying how attuned he was to her every movement.

Nick smiled when he realized that she was staring at him. Darcy analyzed him, trying to guess what he was up to.

"You may step into the kitchen and take a seat, Darcy. I've made some bacon and scrambled eggs, so you're not the main course on the menu today."

Darcy felt the smile in his tone of voice and grimaced. Then she realized that it wasn't the first time she had reacted like that in his presence, and she resented that the man had such a power over her actions.

Moreover, the woman didn't like it when someone made fun of her. That man seemed more than capable of arousing her anger, even though he hadn't wronged her in any way.

Darcy stepped forward into the kitchen and replied, "I haven't thought you'd eat me. I'm not so frightened, you know?"

Her tone was haughty and challenging, and Nick's lips twitched with mirth. Nick shook his head with amusement and bit his lower lip not to burst into laughter.

He turned his head to her and grinned, "You could have fooled me. You've put some pieces together, haven't you? That's good. To be afraid of no matter what is a waste of time. You fight, or you surrender. It's as simple as that."

Darcy narrowed her eyes. '*It's easy for you to say it, you, overbearing giant,*' she thought with resentment.

The man could be mistaken for a bear from afar, and Darcy was tiny compared to him. She couldn't have won in a fight against him. Nick was watching her eyes, so he read her thoughts and chose to reply to her unspoken words.

"Size isn't everything, you know. I recall that women have their own weapons, and sometimes, those are more powerful than the strength of a man."

"It's easy for you to say that when you have nothing to fear," Darcy snapped back. "Do you think I would have looked like this if I'd had those weapons, you are talking about?" Darcy asked Nick in a surly tone of voice, pointing a finger to her face.

Her eyes flashed with unsuppressed anger, and the color raised in her cheeks.

"Maybe you haven't learned to use those weapons, I'm talking about. Or maybe you've met someone who doesn't know anything else but talking with their fists. I'm sorry that such a thing happened to you, but it isn't always like that, you know? One day, you might find a man who can understand something else," Nick shrugged.

"I prefer not to find out what men could understand," she replied in the same disdainful tone of voice. "I have learned enough about men lately. I have especially learned to trust nobody, and in particular a man," Darcy added in a bitter voice.

"Maybe it's better, who knows," Nick answered thoughtfully. "I don't trust anyone either. Or almost anyone," he corrected himself.

Nick remembered that he had some terrific friends. He could put his life in their hands without fear, and they would always have his back if he asked for help.

"It isn't worth the trouble," Nick continued. "Usually, you end up with nothing but problems. But that's me. You shouldn't take me as an example, you know," he shrugged with indifference.

Nick's voice reeked of sadness and sullenness. That made Darcy wonder about what might have happened to him that he turned out so disappointed in the human race. Darcy nurtured her own disillusionment, but hers was more specific. Nick's seemed to encompass a broader range.

The sadness Nick tried to hide proved too much for Darcy, though. She had her own burdens and didn't need anyone else's. The woman's face was expressive, so Nick read her thoughts right away. He gave up talking and came with the pan to the table.

"Would you bring the plates and forks to the table, please? You will find them in that cupboard there," he showed to her, tilting his head in the right direction.

Darcy threw the once-frozen meat into the sink and then brought the plates to the table, where Nick divided the food between the two of them. Then, they took their places and started to eat in silence.

They didn't need any conversation. Now and then, the two people would glance one at the other, but their interaction during breakfast didn't go further than that.

CHAPTER SEVEN

WHEN THEY FINISHED eating and drank their coffee, Nick asked Darcy, "What are you going to do today?"

The young woman kept silent for a few moments, pondering his question. She didn't really know what to do. She had planned to run away, and she had already done that.

After a while, Darcy answered Nick's question, "Actually, I don't know. I suppose I will borrow your t-shirt if you don't mind. I don't have anything else to wear, you know. Then I will go somewhere."

Her clouded eyes told Nick that Darcy didn't have a precise destination in mind. She just thought of wandering around, and that wasn't a brilliant thing to do, especially for someone who didn't know Montana's mountains. Montana was a beautiful but treacherous place. A green person could find their end there, and quite smoothly.

"Do you have anywhere to go?" Nick asked her while he leaned forward and braced his elbows on the top of the table. His brows bunched on his forehead, and his eyes narrowed, observing Darcy.

"No, not really," Darcy shrugged with indifference. "I think I'll find something somewhere," she added pensively.

Nick stared at her for a few long moments. Embarrassed because of his scrutiny, Darcy lowered her eyes.

"I don't mind if you decide to stay around here for a while," Nick said.

"You might as well share some of the household chores with me. There is plenty of food in the pantry. So, that won't be a problem. As you've seen, the rooms are empty. No one lives here but me," Nick waved his hand with negligence. "You can wait for better weather for a while, although the weather might get worse soon, not better."

'*Or you should wait to regain your self-confidence,*' Nick continued silently in his mind because he couldn't speak up his mind. He was sure that Darcy would be furious if she knew what he was actually thinking.

Darcy didn't say anything for a while but gazed at him with suspicion.

"Don't look at me like that," Nick snapped at her. "I don't care about your looks, and anyway, you look like hell right now so that you know. Black and blue never tempted me. I'm not inviting you to share the cottage with me because I want a toy to play with it. I've just thought that you need a refuge. That's all, Darcy. This cottage is empty," he gesticulated. "I have the means, and you have the need. So, I think that things would work just fine for you if you stayed." '*It's not like I need a houseguest,*' Nick continued crossly in his mind.

Darcy nodded after a brief hesitation. She thought that at least she had that lock on the door if any problems appeared. At the same time, the woman had the unsettling feeling that Nick could read her thoughts, and that mortified her more.

"May I ask what you are doing in this deserted land?" Darcy asked him.

"It is not as deserted as you think," Nick retorted, touched by her criticism. "Anyway, I breed horses," he shrugged. "They bring me some money and a lot of satisfaction, and that is enough for me."

Darcy tilted her head and watched him pensively. She understood what Nick was saying. It meant a lot to have satisfaction in one's work, even if one didn't have anything else.

"Maybe I can help you there too," Darcy proposed in a shy tone of voice.

"No way!" Nick interjected more forcefully than he would have liked it.

Nick knew that he was somewhat touchy when it came to his horses. When he didn't care one bit about the rest of his belongings, he was extremely possessive and proud of his stud.

"No one touches my mounts. They might be only a few, but they belong to me. I don't want anyone to get between my horses and me," Nick replied harshly.

That tone of voice came from Nick's guilt. Nick knew that he wasn't entirely honest with Darcy, and that thought nudged at him. The man remembered well enough that he had left someone else to take care of his stud a few times in the past when he headed out of the region and needed help.

"No need to snap at me in a huff," Darcy replied. The woman's brows bunched on her forehead, making Nick think that she looked like an angry kitten.

The man's reaction offended Darcy, and she threw her head back in displeasure. Her nostrils flared, and her lips twitched. She barely stopped the biting words ready to flow out of her mouth.

Darcy was sick of people who thought that she was only a tiny package with some looks but no brain or feelings. People had labeled her that way since she grew a pair of breasts and her hips rounded.

"However, I often worked with horses, and more than once, I worked on a ranch. So that you know," Darcy threw her shaggy ebony hair back off her shoulder with a nervous gesture.

Darcy hadn't forgotten to comb her hair, but she hadn't dared to borrow the man's comb. She had spotted it on the glass shelf under the mirror. However, it felt too intimate to use it, and besides, Darcy didn't want to get onto Nick's wrong side.

Nick's gaze lingered on the woman's wild mane, and amusement crinkled the corners of his eyes for a few seconds. Her petulant gesture reminded Nick of a balky filly. Busy with more pleasant and mundane things, Nick's mind needed time to register the woman's words. Finally, the man's brain processed what Darcy had said, and he bristled at her words.

"And does that make you an expert, or what?" Nick asked with annoyance and straightened his shoulders. He knew that his stance made him look huger. He had done it on purpose. Nick wanted to make Darcy quit bickering with him and thought that his body size would do the trick.

"No, I'm far from an expert, but at least, I know my way around a barn," she replied in an arrogant tone of voice. "Anyway, I think that your testosterone level is way too high, and that's why you can't allow me to work with you in the stables. I am a mere woman, after all. In your opinion, I'm meant to take care of the chores in the house, aren't I?" she replied testily.

Her feisty attitude impressed and bewildered Nick. Darcy had reacted like a scared mouse before then, so he hadn't expected the woman to fight back. Nick had considered that Darcy lost the grit of challenging someone, given the traces of the rough beating she had gone through. She proved him wrong, and that didn't sit well with him.

"I haven't said you should do..." Nick started to say, but she interrupted him.

"You implied," Darcy replied vivaciously. "It's the same thing," she braced her hands on her hips. She was still sitting, so that was quite a feat.

"Don't you ever put words in my mouth, Darcy," Nick snapped back at her. The man jumped off his chair and stepped angrily forward. He clenched his fists, and the muscles in his forearms bunched.

Darcy's eyes widened. She hadn't thought that he would react in any way violently. Despite his impressive figure, Nick hadn't seemed to have anything in common with an angry bear.

Her words didn't upset Nick. He was annoyed because he had misjudged her. The man had seldom been wrong in his past life, and he was afraid that he started slipping now. Nick couldn't afford that.

"If you want to do something in the house, then it is fine with me. If you don't, then it is also fine. But step back and leave me alone. That's all I ask from you," Nick added in a biting tone of voice. The man already regretted his loss of temper. The flicker of fear in Darcy's eyes nudged at him.

Darcy didn't reply. She just picked up the dirty dishes and took them to the working table. The woman crossed the kitchen floor with angry strides, and Nick's eyes followed the gentle moves of her generous hips. The man couldn't say that he didn't like what he saw.

Darcy threw the dishes into the sink, and the noise reverberated throughout the room. Nick's left brow lifted in surprise. He hadn't believed her capable of that either. Nick wondered where the scared bunny had disappeared. The woman had changed right under his eyes.

Darcy didn't care if the plates broke or got chipped, and she didn't care about the loud noise. The woman merely shrugged and then turned to Nick again with a defiant look on her face.

"You should know that I'm not very good at that," the woman informed Nick in a challenging tone of voice.

Darcy braced her hands on her hips once more and stared Nick down. She held her back straight, and that threw her rounded breasts forward.

Involuntarily, Nick's eyes zeroed in on her chest for a few moments. Afterward, he shook his head to clear his mind, and his gaze shifted up to her face. Bewilderment clouded his eyes.

"At what?" Nick asked. He didn't know what she wanted to say.

"Household chores," Darcy replied peevishly. "I've worked mostly outside the house so far. I have little experience with housework. I don't know to cook either," she pointed out.

"It doesn't really matter," Nick replied to her, waving his hand indifferently. "I am not interested in hiring a maid. I've just thought to give you something to do. I don't care if you can't do it, or you don't want to do it," the man shrugged with indifference. "I can do everything by myself. I've done it so far, after all," he lifted his shoulders once more.

Nick tilted his head and pondered upon the implications of her words some more. Then he said, "However, it would have been nice if you cooked. You have already tasted the heights of my cooking. Eh, anyway, at least we'll eat."

Nick shrugged with indifference.

"You can just stay as a guest in my house for as long as it takes. You need to recover first. And I'm not speaking only about the bruises on your face, or any other wounds you might have on your body. I hope you can catch my drift," Nick added with another wave of his hand toward her face and body.

Darcy blushed ashamed. The man merely wanted to help her, and she behaved like a catty woman. Darcy nodded to him and then went back to the sink, flexing her fists. She started doing the dishes without another word.

Nick watched her pensively for a few moments. Then, he shrugged once more and headed to the door.

Nick felt like he should have said something to reassure her, but he couldn't find the right words. However, before going out, he informed her, "I'll probably be back at noon."

CHAPTER EIGHT

THE ENTRANCE DOOR CLOSED quietly behind Nick. Then, Darcy relaxed her body and sighed with relief. She was finally alone.

Darcy flexed her shoulders to work the kinks out of them, and then she straightened and dried her hands on a kitchen towel thrown negligently on the worktable. Darcy wasn't as apprehensive with Nick as she had been with Emmett. Nick seemed harmless enough, at least toward her. Still, his departure brought her a measure of peace.

Darcy took a deep breath and smoothed the t-shirt on her hips with slow gestures. She didn't know what to do with the time she had on her hands now. To relax entirely was out of the question. Darcy didn't believe that she would ever forget what had happened to her, and she couldn't feel at ease, especially in a stranger's house.

Blood hummed in her veins, and Darcy needed a vigorous activity to get rid of her anger. It had been eating her up for days.

The woman turned all sorts of ideas in her head, but none seemed practical. With resignation, Darcy decided to do something in the house.

She didn't relish what waited in store for her. Quite the opposite. The young woman hated housework chores. She did them but grudgingly, and only because she couldn't stand disorder or dirt in her living quarters.

First, Darcy looked around the house with a critical eye. The cottage wasn't dirty, but it wasn't spic and span either. It seemed in dire need of the hand of a woman. She could see evidence that Nick had done his best, but his best didn't meet her standards.

Darcy shook her head in dismay and started looking for a vacuum cleaner. However, she had to give up her quest soon.

Nick didn't seem interested in small luxuries, like a vacuum cleaner or even a toaster. The man didn't own any appliances, besides the antique stove in the kitchen and the washer and dryer upstairs. With another sigh, Darcy thought to find a broom. She hadn't seen any.

'What the heck? At least, he must have a broom in this god-forsaken cottage,' Darcy reflected with exasperation. She had looked in all the typical places and found nothing. The woman spent another half an hour looking for that darn broom and stumbled on it in the last place she would have imagined. The brush and a pale green dustpan leaned on the exterior wall of the cottage on the porch.

Darcy sent a few sweet thoughts in Nick's direction, mumbling to herself with annoyance. She had already lost a lot of time and most of her endurance.

She swept the rooms diligently, but her thoughts returned to Nick all the time. Darcy wondered what kind of man didn't own a vacuum cleaner in the twenty-first century, even if he lived in a remote area in Montana.

PULLED IN

That thing said a lot about the man who had opened his house to her without too many questions. Darcy concluded that she should look into Nick's life a little more attentively. She didn't want to get into the same situation she had been with Emmett.

Now, Darcy knew that appearances misled. Emmett had seemed a gentleman through and through, and in the end, he proved that he was nothing else but a brutal thug. She hoped that Nick would turn out being different. However, she preferred to be cautious and decided that a thorough search through cabinets and drawers was in order. She had never searched in someone else's house before, but tough times required severe measures.

Darcy's idea of rummaging through the house and learn about Nick had a brief life, though. She found most of the drawers locked and didn't discover anything to uncover the man's mystery in the ones that were unlocked.

The bedroom betrayed only his disinterest in fashion and fancy clothes. The man owned a couple of blue jeans and an armful of t-shirts and flannel shirts. Darcy also found a couple of pairs of worn-out working boots, a pair of good leather shoes, and some sneakers under his bed.

She had already visited the bathroom and noticed that Nick wasn't a fan of expensive aftershave or other cosmetic products. Not that the man would have shaved regularly. The stubble on the bear's face proved his aversion toward shaving.

Darcy had already seen the kitchen and pantry, and the two rooms didn't hold any secrets. She had checked the basement while looking for a vacuum cleaner. However, Darcy hadn't seen anything but a working bench and a closet with a latch on it, so she couldn't have a look inside the locker.

The one unlocked drawer in Nick's study sheltered a bunch of documents. They held some historical value, but nothing in that drawer helped Darcy to figure out her host. Darcy pursed her lips and stomped her foot to the floor. She hated it when she didn't succeed in her endeavors.

With a groan, she threw her hands in the air and resigned to return to that cursed broom, she had chased practically all morning. And yet, her mind turned around, filled with questions. Nick had aroused her curiosity, besides her need to know and understand the man in whose house she resided for the moment.

CHAPTER NINE

NICK SLOWED DOWN AND jumped off his mount. With a loving gesture, he tapped the powerful neck of the svelte filly he had been riding for a couple of hours and led her toward the pen he had built on one side of his ranch. A gush of wind ruffled his hair, and he looked up.

The sun was high in the sky and shone brightly. However, angry clouds gathered from the west and advanced slowly to that part of the mountain.

The smell in the air warned Nick that rain would come soon, and he shrugged with indifference. He had already trained all his horses, so the storm wouldn't be a hindrance or slow him down.

Nick rubbed the back of his neck, trying to ease off the aches in his stiff neck, shoulders. Tension had knotted his muscles. Nick had worked hard since morning without a break unless he counted the moments between changing the mounts when he drank some water.

Nick had told Darcy that he would be back at noon, but he didn't return to the cottage. He preferred to work.

Darcy's presence put stupid ideas in his head, and besides, he didn't feel like going through a new discussion with her.

Besides, Nick wasn't in a particularly good mood as he hadn't had much sleep the night before. The man had remained awake and listened to the sobs coming from Darcy's room. His heart had cringed, and his fists had clenched in quiet rage. Nick hadn't fallen asleep until the wee hours of the morning, and he felt the effects of his brief sleep now.

Nick wondered what Darcy was doing, and his eyes turned toward the house again. Unconsciously, the man had been doing that all morning.

Now and then, Nick had caught a glimpse of the woman. Darcy was moving around, either busy cleaning or just wandering around with a specific purpose, the man couldn't even fathom.

Anyway, apparently, Darcy had decided to go over the entire house. Nick knew that she had the work cut out for her, and her actions made him feel guilty somewhat, mainly because he had mentioned the household chores at breakfast.

Nick reckoned that he hadn't bothered with the cottage much. He had kept it clean, but he didn't get too anal about it. His priorities laid somewhere else.

The proximity of the stables to the cottage made it easy for him to keep track of Darcy's movements. Nick had built the barns not far from the ranch house because he wanted to keep a close eye on his horses. If he had made the stables farther down the road, he would have worried about his stock all the time. He couldn't have slept at night if he hadn't had complete control over his stud's safety.

Darcy went inside the house again, and Nick returned to his work. He led the golden filly into the pen, where he let the horses run free, and took off the saddle, draping it over the fence.

Nick had built the barns not far from the ranch house because he wanted to keep a close eye on his horses. If he had made the stables farther down the road, he would have worried about his stock all the time. He couldn't have slept at night if he hadn't had complete control over his stud's safety.

Nick cooled the horse down, rubbing the mare's fur with a bunch of herbs. He finished brushing her mane and slapped the horse's flank. The filly ran and joined her friends, who were enjoying the seeds and water that Nick had prepared for them earlier.

Nick turned to carry the saddle back into the tack room when the gallop of horses coming up the hill reached him. His ranch was way out of the beaten trails, so he didn't hear that often around there.

Nick frowned for a moment and put the seat back on the fence. He assumed a relaxed stance, but his attention sharpened. An experienced eye would have observed that the man was far from being relaxed. Nick was, in fact, getting ready to confront an enemy or more if he had to.

Six riders crossed the meadow, and Nick recognized Emmett Driscoll and his people immediately.

The man had a black reputation in that area of Montana. In no time at all, Emmett Driscoll had become the enemy of two-thirds of the inhabitants in the county. The other third of the population wasn't aware yet that the sniveling man just waited patiently to grab their lands from under their feet and throw them out of their houses. Nick knew that it wouldn't be long until they saw Driscoll for what he really was.

Nick had never understood how people could wallow in a feeling of false security. He, for one, kept a sharp eye on Emmett Driscoll's dealings.

Nick surveyed the riders through narrowed eyes. As a rule, Nick didn't like any impromptu visits from anyone. Driscoll had been on his blacklist from the moment the man moved into the area.

Nick had never welcomed Emmett Driscoll in the county, and he hadn't made a secret that he didn't expect any visits from the man. Driscoll had had his eyes on Nick's ranch for some time now, and still, he hadn't succeeded in buying Nick's land or chase him out of the region yet.

Driscoll's presence on his territory made Nick wonder about the man's reasons. Nick's ranch was far away from Driscoll's grounds, so the man rarely passed that way.

Emmett Driscoll led the pack of riders with the aura of a king surveying his domain, and that angered Nick. He would have liked to throw the man off his horse. But then, Nick was a prudent man and weighed his moves with care. For the moment, he decided to merely watch the men and take a stand only if it became necessary.

Emmett Driscoll's shoulder-long blond hair touched his collar, and his white shirt already showed wet patches. The humidity of the day had affected him. Driscoll had lost some of the impeccable appearance he liked to display in front of the world. That thought made the corners of Nick's mouth twitch in a repressed grin.

PULLED IN

Driscoll's hair looked wind-blown, although his wide-brimmed hat covered most of his head. Apparently, the man had ridden his mount hard. The horse showed signs of fatigue, and his hide shone with sweat. Driscoll clearly had a vital purpose of riding so far out of his regular paths.

The wide brim of Driscoll's hat hid the man's eyes, but Nick remembered well their slanted form and green color. He didn't need a reminder just then. Still, it would have been nice if he could have read the man's eyes.

The riders stopped right before the fence, but Nick didn't abandon his treacherously relaxed stance. Driscoll touched the brim of his cowboy hat in a lame attempt to politeness, and his gesture lacked sincerity. The line of his mouth showed that he didn't enjoy seeing Nick. The feeling was mutual, though, so Nick didn't mind.

The other five men didn't move a muscle. They sat in their saddles with their backs straight and stared Nick down. The men tried to intimidate him with their eyes and the bulk of their bodies. Nick remembered that it was a known fact that Driscoll chose only burly men to join his guards.

Nick didn't make any effort to welcome them but just nodded curtly toward the group. He didn't care for the men's cockiness and didn't intend to let them have the upper hand.

"Do you have any business around, Driscoll?" Nick asked the leader of the group in a harsh tone of voice.

Nick had learned that it was necessary to show toughness when dealing with bullies. Otherwise, they would have walked all over him.

"No need to get your hackles up, man," Driscoll replied, his voice as harsh as Nick's.

The man was actually fed up, and at Nick's audacity, his annoyance went up a notch. Nick had been a thorn in Emmett Driscoll's side for a long time, and Emmett counted the days until he could get rid of the man. He couldn't wait to throw Nick off the mountain.

Emmett would have liked to take care of Nick right then, but that wasn't the day to do it. He had more urgent matters to solve. Emmett had been riding around for hours and hadn't found a trace of Darcy. Tired and hungry, he didn't feel like diplomatically asking questions anymore.

"My girlfriend's got lost in the woods, apparently," Emmett said and wiped his mouth with his sleeve.

That was the story he had been saying around the entire day. He couldn't divulge the fact that '*his girlfriend*' had actually run away from him in the dead of night.

"She went out for a short walk this morning and hadn't come back. The woman doesn't know the forest. You know how the city girls are," he tried to joke, but the dryness of his tone swallowed the humor out of his words. "I'm afraid she doesn't know to find her way back. Haven't you seen her? She's petite, dark-haired, blue-eyed..." Emmett explained. An uptight smile perched on his lips.

'*I bet you'd like to find her, you, asshole,*' Nick thought, and anger hummed in his veins. Now, he had a better understanding of Darcy's bruises. Nick wouldn't have put it beyond Emmett to pummel a powerless woman.

Nick shook his head and puckered his lips. "No one passed by here this morning," he replied with a straight face. '*And I am not even lying,*' he thought. Indeed, no one had passed by that day.

The men measured him up but couldn't read a thing on Nick's face.

"Maybe she got into your house," Emmett advanced the idea. "If she was scared and tired..."

"I doubt it," Nick interrupted him and shrugged with negligence. "I would have seen her. I've been here most of the time. But, hey, if you need to make sure, you can go and check," he continued with blatant indifference. "Be my guest. I don't mind. I still have things to do around here, though. You'll have to let yourself inside. The door is open," Nick warned him and picked up the saddle, he had draped on the fence earlier.

Nick turned his back on the men and headed toward the tack room with purposeful steps. However, he didn't trust any of them, so he didn't take his attention from the group.

Nick didn't worry about Darcy. He had already seen her taking advantage of the men's position with their backs to the ranch house. Darcy had tiptoed out of the cottage and gone around the corner to the barn situated behind the house.

Nick sighed. He imagined that Darcy wanted to hide or run away. He would have to go after her once Emmett Driscoll left. Nick couldn't let her get lost in the forest for real.

Emmett watched Nick's figure and tilted his head. He had the itching that Nick was lying to him, although he couldn't say why. Nick had looked utterly disinterested in their quest and didn't seem to care if they ransacked his cottage either.

Nick couldn't have done anything if Emmett decided to vandalize his lodge, but Emmett didn't want to do it just yet. He had some particular plans in store for Nick. The man had been a constant source of annoyance for Driscoll for a long while.

'*Soon enough... Soon enough*,' the man reflected. The time to put those plans into practice would come. First, Emmett needed to solve the complication that Darcy's presence had caused.

The man took off his hat with a nervous gesture and wiped his forehead with his forearm. He restored the hat on his head and turned to his people. "Come, let's move," he said and steered his mount toward the ranch house.

His men followed him. However, the biggest one of them took the time to glance back at Nick with menacing eyes.

When he reached the cottage, Emmett got closer and looked inside through the windows, but didn't see any trace of the wayward woman. The man spat furiously and swore.

Emmett had been almost sure that he would find Darcy there. He pulled the reins, and with a guttural sound, he steered his mount toward the slope of the mountain to cross to the West Butte.

Nick slowly turned around and watched the men until they vanished into the forest. He didn't trust them not to come back and hurried to leave the saddle inside the tackle room. Then he came out and scanned the surrounding area thoroughly.

Nick moved toward the ranch house only when he was sure that Emmett Driscoll and his men wouldn't come back. He didn't doubt that he should expect another visit from them once they wouldn't find Darcy anywhere. However, for the moment, he judged that it was safe enough to go and search for the woman.

PULLED IN

Nick headed with huge strides toward the barn behind the cottage. The door of the barn was only half-closed, and he feared that Emmett might have noticed it. However, Driscoll hadn't stopped, and that was encouraging.

Nick advanced but took care to make noise and warn Darcy that he was coming. He didn't feel like being hit with a blunt object over the head. The man remembered well Darcy's fear from the night before. He knew that she had reasons if Emmett Driscoll had left those signs over her body.

Emmett Driscoll was a vicious man. Even though Nick didn't interact with people a lot, he still went down to town for a drink now and then. The whispers saying that Driscoll had roughened a few women who used to sell their charms for a fist of money had reached Nick's ears. Those rumors had made Nick sick at the time. Now, thinking of Emmett's strong hands touching Darcy's pale and silky skin, Nick gnashed his teeth.

"Darcy, it's me, Nick. You can come out now. They've left," he announced and pushed the door of the barn open.

The light filtered through the opening, and moths flew in the air. Nick came from the bright light of the sun, so he didn't see anything for a few seconds until his eyes got used to the shadows in the building. Nick waited but didn't receive any answer to his call. He listened carefully, and the sound of a light breath lifted the corners of his mouth.

Nick localized Darcy's position immediately. She had hunched behind the sacks with grains, he kept in the far-left corner.

"Come on, Darcy, it is safe to come out. Driscoll has left, and he took his goons with him," Nick said in a reassuring tone of voice, trying to persuade the woman to abandon her hide-out.

The sound of shuffling feet told him that Darcy had chosen to believe him. Yet, she didn't hurry to come out. She took her time to reach the front of the barn, but Nick waited patiently.

CHAPTER TEN

A FAINT BLUSH POWDERED the top of Darcy's cheekbones when she looked up to Nick. Her eyes met the man's intense gaze, and her lips quivered at the intensity shining in his pupils.

"Driscoll has left," Nick said once more, while his gaze searched Darcy's face carefully.

He noticed that the woman was scared out of her mind, and the paleness of her face worried him. Even her lips had turned almost white.

"But they'll be back," Darcy replied quietly. She clenched her hands together so that the man couldn't see that they shook. She couldn't control her fear and felt ashamed.

"Yes, they will be back," Nick admitted softly and nodded.

Darcy tried to see what Nick was thinking, but an impenetrable light shone in the man's dark brown eyes.

"I should go away," she whispered after a few seconds as if she talked to herself.

And yet, Nick heard her words and pursed his mouth. "I don't think it is wise," he replied and shook his head to give more power to his words.

Then he braced his hands on his hips. "I think you'd better tell me what's going on," Nick urged Darcy to open up to him.

However, his invitation sounded more like order in her ears, and Darcy cringed.

"I might be able to help," Nick explained his reasons for demanding her trust. "You have no chance alone out there in the forest. You were lucky enough that a bobcat didn't decide to have you for a snack the other day," the man observed in a harsh tone of voice now.

Nick had already understood that Darcy must have crossed on foot the entire expanse of ground between Driscoll's house and his cottage.

He couldn't believe that the woman had survived the trip. Something serious must have happened to force the woman to brave the unknown and the dangers lurking on the mountain, and that angered him.

"You can't help me," Darcy shook her head stubbornly. "I don't think anyone can. You don't know Emmett," she explained in a resigned tone of voice.

"As a matter of fact, I do know Emmett Driscoll," Nick contradicted Darcy. "I don't think there's anyone around here who doesn't know him or of him. So, if I offer my help, it means that I know how to deal with a man like him," Nick reassured her in a firm voice.

His tone of voice didn't leave room for contradiction. Yet, Darcy didn't dare to believe him, even though she had never wanted anything as much as that.

Still, Darcy knew that Nick had already helped her more than enough. She didn't want to put the man in any danger. At least, not in more danger than he already was. Darcy had read Emmett's body language correctly. It didn't escape her notice that the man loathed Nick with a passion.

PULLED IN

Darcy stared at the giant before her eyes and tried to find the correct words to explain her reasons for acting that way.

She wanted to let him down gently. The man didn't deserve her cattiness, although Darcy definitely felt quite raw right then. She had to choose her words carefully so that she didn't come across as ungrateful.

Nevertheless, anxiety screamed inside her chest. The rhythm of her heartbeat filled her ears, and she couldn't focus enough to order her ideas.

Nick closed the space between the two of them and put his arm around the woman's shoulders carefully. He didn't want to frighten her. Then, he gently steered her toward the door of the barn.

"Let's go inside the house and talk. I think a glass of whiskey is in order, even though it is not five yet," Nick tried to make a joke and lighten Darcy's mood. And yet, Nick did believe that Darcy needed a shot of whiskey to recover. He gazed at her intently. The woman resembled a ghost with her inky black hair and pallid skin.

Darcy lowered her eyes. What she read in Nick's eyes made her feel weird things in her belly. The man gave her the impression that he cared about her, but she, for one, didn't believe that people cared about others anymore.

Darcy bit her lower lip, and her mind attempted frantically to navigate through the contrary feelings and thoughts she experienced. And still, her feet moved one in front of the other in the direction that Nick had chosen.

They stepped out of the barn, and Darcy blinked. The brightness of the day hurt her eyes. She had always shown sensitivity to the light of the sun. Besides, her eyes had adjusted to the darkness in the barn.

Nick noticed Darcy's discomfort but kept silent. He continued to direct her on the shingle path, which led toward the house.

Halfway there, Nick glanced at the sky toward the west and noticed the puffy clouds gathered on the line of the horizon. He knew the signs. They would be in for a severe storm in less than an hour.

The man ground his teeth in frustration. Nick didn't want to rush his discussion with Darcy, but at the same time, he needed to take care of his horses first. He had to shelter them before the storm broke and make sure that they had everything they needed until the following morning.

The signs showed that the storm would last for at least a few hours, if not more. The darkness of the western sky and the eerie light preceding that thick grayish blanket of clouds announced heavy and prolonged rainfalls.

Nick had learned that the heavens wouldn't quiet down before dawn the following day if the horizon looked like that. He had witnessed some powerful thunderstorms on that side of the mountain and didn't take them lightly.

Darcy looked up at Nick's profile just in time to see his frown. She caught her lower lip between her teeth and thought of an apology. "I know I am a bother, Nick," Darcy started to say.

PULLED IN

The man stopped abruptly. His arm, anchored around her shoulders, brought her to a halt as well, so Darcy couldn't finish what she wanted to say. She felt that Nick had turned toward her, so she lifted her eyes to him.

"What the heck made you think that I would consider you a bother?" Nick asked her in a quarrelsome tone of voice, and that made her lower her eyes again. The man had enough on his mind and didn't feel like tiptoeing around Darcy all the time, especially when she came up with such stupid ideas.

Darcy bit her lower lip again. She dared to sneak another gaze up to Nick's face from under her lashes. The tight line of his mouth and his eyebrows bunched together made her turn her eyes back to the ground.

"You are definitely upset," Darcy murmured almost inaudibly. "As we are alone here, you must be upset with me," she continued afterward in a stronger tone of voice than Nick would have expected. Darcy reacted like a scaredy-cat almost all the time and surprised him whenever she found her gumption.

"Actually, you are wrong," Nick replied to her in a softer voice. "I'm not upset with you, and you're not a bother. Do you see those clouds over there?" he pointed toward the horizon.

Darcy chanced a look at the sky and noticed the angry grey blanket for the first time. Surprised, she took a step back, and her eyes widened. Her lips parted, and the woman took a deep breath. Afterward, she licked her lips anxiously.

"I've never seen such a dense bank of clouds," the woman replied with bewilderment after a few seconds.

"Well, you've seen it now," Nick remarked dryly. "The problem is that I have to take care of my horses. That will probably take about thirty minutes," he informed her, gazing straight into her eyes. "So, I'm afraid that our discussion must wait until then. However, I want you with me where I can keep an eye on you and see what happens to you all the time," Nick added and steered Darcy toward the stables. "When I have finished, we will go back to the cottage and talk," he decided in a deadpan tone of voice.

Darcy would have liked to contradict him, but she didn't miss the steel underlining his voice, so she decided to keep quiet. Besides, she preferred being with him. Nick gave her a certain sense of safety.

Nick hurried and forced Darcy to take longer strides. "We're close to the stables," Nick told her. "Once there, you should go into the tack room. There's a chair in there," Nick explained to Darcy. "You needn't stand and watch me. I think you're tired enough."

"But I'd like to help you," Darcy replied in a weak voice, afraid of his reply. The young woman remembered that Nick had already refused her once that morning, and she didn't expect that he had changed his mind.

Nick's impulse was to give her a sharp reply, but then, he glanced at her and couldn't utter the words. The hopeful glow in Darcy's eyes stopped him, and he decided to give her a gentle answer.

"Not this time, sweetheart. You are too tired for such hard work. Don't forget that you had crossed the woods yesterday, and you didn't sleep enough last night."

PULLED IN

A blush spread all over Darcy's face, and Nick said, "I heard you. But there's nothing to be ashamed of," he pointed out.

"I am pretty sure you've been through a lot. And right now, I have to move fast. Besides, my horses don't know you, and most of them are fanciful. They'll need some time to get used to you," Nick explained to Darcy in a kind tone of voice and brushed the tips of his fingers over her shoulder.

Darcy shuddered slightly under his touch, and he stepped back. "Let's go," he nudged her to move with a wave of his hand.

Nick started before her with determined steps, and Darcy followed, trying to match his strides. At the stable, Nick pointed toward the tack room, but Darcy shook her head with obstinacy.

She preferred to stay outside and watch him working with the horses, so she braced her elbows over the fence of the enclosure and her right leg on the lower wooden log.

Nick shrugged and didn't comment. With a last glance at the sky, he rushed to gather his horses and cool them down. A couple of them were extremely finicky, so Nick had his work cut for him to make them retire inside the stable before their usual time.

When the first furious raindrops fell, Nick was just bedding the last of his horses for the night. The sky had already darkened. An eerie translucent light had spread at the edges of the black blanket that covered the horizon.

Darcy abandoned her spot near the fence and ran inside the stable. There, she waited near a stall, petting a stallion on the head. Darcy had already made friends with most of the horses. However, a couple of temperamental mares refused to accept her with stubbornness.

"We're done here," Nick came to Darcy and caught her hand in his. "Let's go back to the cottage," he said, without a glance at her. Nick imagined that his gesture might have scared her, and he didn't want to witness her anxiety. Nick's big palm swallowed Darcy's small hand utterly. In spite of that, the woman didn't feel menaced by his touch.

Darcy had thought that she wouldn't ever be able to allow another man to get so close to her. Apparently, she had been wrong. She didn't feel any anxiety when Nick's fingers covered hers, or when the man pulled her after him.

CHAPTER ELEVEN

DARCY AND NICK RAN into the ranch house and laughed heartily. Raindrops clung to their lashes and shone in their hair. They had crossed the last forty yards under a relentless deluge, and now they were both soaked to the bones.

Darcy shook her head to get rid of most of the water in her hair. Still, wet locks glued to her skin and covered her eyes.

Nick brushed the wayward curls off her face with the tips of his fingers, and Darcy's smile froze on her lips at his tender gesture. Wide-eyed, she stared at Nick with the look of a doe caught in the headlights of a car.

Nick's hand fell immediately, and the man stepped back. He avoided her eyes artfully. He shifted his eyes over her shoulder and said, "I am going to light the fire in the living room. You should take a towel and dry yourself. I think I left one in the blue hamper in the bathroom upstairs. If I remember correctly, I also left a bigger t-shirt there, and you could borrow it," Nick dared to glance at Darcy.

"I guess that the shirt will cover your body at least up to the knees, if not more."

The young woman glanced furtively at him and dipped her head immediately. However, she chose not to reply but merely nodded. Darcy had noticed that her t-shirt was glued to her breasts and hips and showed off all the interesting spots in between, so she rushed upstairs. She didn't imagine that Nick could have missed any of that.

A smile flourished on Nick's mouth at the sound of Darcy's quick steps on the first floor, and the man brushed his fingers through his wet hair with a nervous gesture.

He shook his head and then strode toward the fireplace to make a fire, as he had promised.

Darcy returned downstairs and found Nick busy at the stove, already preparing some hot coffee for both of them. The man turned his head toward Darcy's steps and said, "I thought we should mix coffee with whiskey. Both would help."

At his words, Darcy stopped in the middle of the kitchen. She had no idea what to do or what answer to give him. Moreover, she felt conspicuous dressed only in Nick's t-shirt.

Nick had been right in his assessment. The top did cover Darcy's knees. However, to her annoyance, it dipped dangerously over her breasts. It displayed her impressive charms more than she would have liked it.

"Why don't you take a seat at the table?" Nick invited her in a quiet tone of voice. "I'll be only a couple of minutes more," he explained.

Nick returned to his ministrations with the coffee pot. The coffee had just started to boil, and the man didn't want to splatter the stove. He remembered that Darcy had worked diligently to clean it that morning, and Nick's cooking machine had never shone so brightly before.

Darcy hurried to sit down and made another futile attempt to gather the top above her breasts. At the same time, the young woman was painfully aware of Nick's every move.

Suddenly, she remembered the purpose of the conversation Nick had proposed, and she dreaded what would follow. Darcy knew that she had to tell Nick everything if only to keep him safe. He deserved to know what to expect.

However, she imagined that the man would choose the easy way out after hearing her explanations about what had happened with Emmett.

Any sane man would do the same, after all, and Darcy couldn't condemn Nick for that. She couldn't ask him to get involved in a battle that didn't belong to him.

Nick came to the table with two mugs half-filled with coffee. He put one before Darcy and one before his seat and then left the room. Darcy listened carefully, and the sound of the man's steps told her that Nick headed toward the salon. He returned soon enough with a pot-bellied bottle in his hand.

Nick poured a generous portion of double malt whiskey in Darcy's cup, and then he filled his mug to the rim.

He screwed the lid back to the bottle and hesitated for a second. However, after a second thought, the man decided to leave the whiskey on the table. Nick was sure that they would need some later. The subject of their discussion was Emmett Driscoll, so they would need something powerful to swallow it.

Darcy toyed with the handle of her mug. Her eyes focused on the pattern of the vinyl tablecloth, intent not to meet Nick's dark pupils. However, she sensed that Nick was observing her.

"Why won't you drink some?" Nick inquired in a mild tone of voice and tilted his head toward her mug.

Darcy seemed jumpy, and he thought to make her feel at ease. He understood her reaction. She was probably scared of what she had to divulge.

Darcy nodded and sipped from her cup, holding it between her hands. Apprehension had left her hands cold, so she welcomed the warmth of the mug. Nonetheless, Darcy still couldn't gather her courage to look up at Nick.

Nick watched her musingly and sipped from his cup again. The potent liquid hit the back of his throat and reached his belly. Heat spread through his entire body, and the man forgot utterly about his wet clothes. He hadn't bothered to change or at least dry himself with a towel.

"I think you'd better tell me about everything that happened," Nick nudged Darcy kindly, unwilling to scare her off.

"I will," she murmured hesitantly. Indecision lurked in her tone of voice. Darcy already felt deserted. She knew that Nick would ask her to walk away once he found out why she got to his house. No rational man would have taken upon him the solving of her problems, and Nick wouldn't shelter her in such circumstances either.

"Maybe you should change your clothes, as well," she proposed when she chanced to look up at him. Only now she noticed that Nick's hair was still damp, and his shirt had stuck to his chest.

'*And that's not a bad-looking chest, Darcy,*' she told herself and licked her lips unconsciously.

Without shame, her keen eyes analyzed the ridges of Nick's muscles underlined by the wet cloth. Darcy had rarely seen such broad and well-defined pectorals and biceps on a man.

Nick just shrugged and said, "That's not important. I'm all right, don't worry."

"I'd feel better if you changed," Darcy insisted. She did want to delay the inevitable, but her request wasn't entirely selfish. Darcy didn't want that Nick got sick because of her.

"If you insist," Nick stood up. "But I'll be back in a couple of minutes, Darcy. You should be prepared to talk then," he warned Darcy, throwing a meaningful glance at her.

The woman nodded, and a blush suffused her face. Indeed, her tactic was devised to delay the outcome, but Darcy had hoped that Nick wouldn't be the wiser.

Darcy sipped from her mug broodingly until Nick returned. He had changed in another cotton shirt, but he hadn't bothered to button it to the top. Evidently, the tanned skin stretched over the man's broad chest attracted Darcy's eyes like a magnet.

Nick's lips twitched. It wasn't as if he didn't bother to button the shirt on purpose. Yet, he didn't mind the result. Darcy's reactions at his physic fed the man's ego, and Nick enjoyed her undivided attention. Nick sat down again and gulped most of the coffee he had doctored with whiskey.

"Now, can you tell me what happened?" he inquired, leaning forward and bracing his elbows on the top of the kitchen table.

Darcy nodded but still didn't say anything. Nick had had enough of her evasions and invited her to talk with an impatient wave of his hand.

"I'm just trying to gather my thoughts," Darcy snapped at him. "Just be patient."

'What's there to gather?" Nick shrugged. "Things are as simple as that: how you met Driscoll, how you got to live at his house, and what happened there that made you run away," Nick pointed out, counting on his fingers.

His high-handed manner annoyed Darcy, and she scowled at him. "Well, things are never as easy as that," Darcy replied with irritation. "Everything is a bit more complicated. You need to look at the entire picture," she pointed out.

The woman picked up her mug to sip but noticed that there was nothing inside and grimaced.

Nick stood up with a sigh and brought the coffee pot to the table. He poured some into Darcy's cup and topped it up with whiskey. Then Nick dropped into his chair with a thump and waved his fingers at Darcy to make her talk.

Darcy pursed her lips for a second, and then she drank a mouthful from her cup. She put her cup back onto the table and continued with her story.

"My mother and I mostly navigate the world of horse races. After my father's death, my mother made friends, let's say, with a man or another involved in that world. Unfortunately, her relationships never lasted."

She sipped from her cup and continued, "I think my mother gets bored easily, and besides, she does like to ask for a lot of things. So, men run away pretty fast," Darcy explained, circling her hand in the air.

The woman wanted to clarify her background. However, Darcy was also a little nervous because she couldn't read anything in Nick's eyes. Whenever she got agitated, she would speak faster and gesticulate wildly.

Darcy took a break from telling her story and dipped her lips in her cup once more. Her mouth had already got dry, and Darcy wondered how long it would take to explain everything in that rhythm.

"Anyway," the woman continued afterward, "Mother took me with her to a party a few months ago. There, she met a group of men who seem to possess serious financial means. My mother had been trying to breach such a group for a long time, you see," Darcy explained, leaning forward as if she imparted a terrible secret. 'She had always hoped to find a rich man one day. He would take a fancy to her and then would pamper her and keep her in his world," Darcy pointed her words with broad gestures.

"So, she saw her dream come true," Nick observed in a blunt tone of voice. He had never had a good impression about women who would chase a man for his bank account.

"In a way," Darcy admitted morosely. "Although I don't know how long it will last, especially after my sting with Emmett," she confessed.

"What do you mean?" Nick frowned and drained his mug in one go. He picked up the whiskey bottle and poured some in his cup, but he didn't take his eyes off Darcy.

The woman had blushed violently and seemed slightly embarrassed. Nick just knew that he wouldn't like what she had to say next.

"Well, the guy my mother got involved with is Emmett's friend. He told her that Emmett was interested in me. Mother insisted that I made Emmett's acquaintance, and she even ordered me to make him fall in love with me. Mother bothered me for a few weeks, and I said yes, merely to get rid of her nagging," Darcy admitted.

"You weren't interested," Nick concluded, although Darcy could see that he didn't really believe her.

"No, I wasn't. Emmett looked like a gentleman, but there was no spark if you know what I mean," she explained.

"I'm not a teenager anymore, far from it," the young woman laughed bitterly. Darcy knew that she approached her thirtieth birthday fast. "But still, I do want to feel something for a man I get involved with," she said with irritation. She emphasized her words by tapping her index finger onto the top of the table.

"I see," Nick said without expressing what he really thought.

Darcy just shrugged. It didn't really matter whether Nick believed her or not. After all, the woman was almost sure that he would ask her to leave his cottage once she finished her story. So, she just continued to tell him what happened.

"Anyway, I'll give you the short version. After a few dates, Emmett, supported by my mother, convinced me to visit his ranch. He promised not to ask for anything I wasn't ready to give him. I had been there for about a week when he offered me his card and told me that I should go shopping in Chester. I returned earlier than I was told because I didn't find too much to do in town. You know how that town is," Darcy opened her arms widely. "Anyway, I don't like to spend on useless things, and especially, I can't spend someone else's money. Of course,

I don't have too much money myself so... Anyway, I came back just in time to surprise Emmett closing a deal by killing someone," she said, looking straight into Nick's eyes.

"I see," Nick said, and his eyes turned impenetrable. "What kind of a deal?" he inquired in a hard tone of voice.

"I am not very sure I understood correctly, but I think it involved human trafficking. From what I heard, the deal fell off because Emmett considered that '*the merchandise wasn't of the quality he was told, and he didn't accept to be ripped off.* I'm trying to quote what he said," Darcy specified so that Nick didn't misunderstand.

"And when did he realize that you witnessed everything?" Nick asked her.

"Just after he said that and killed the other guy," Darcy replied quietly.

"I understand now," Nick said and poured some whiskey in his cup with a swift gesture. He drank it in one go and asked, "What happened next?"

Darcy's eyes filled with tears instantly, and Nick barely stopped a groan. He clenched his teeth hard and flexed his fists.

Darcy shook her head and pressed the back of her hands to her eyes. After a few seconds, she dropped her hands onto the table and looked back at Nick.

"I apologize, Nick. I didn't mean to..."

"No problem," Nick replied. "Just go on," he waved his fingers.

"I thought I would be able to tell you everything without all this drama," Darcy explained. "Anyway, Emmett beat me first. Then he raped me and beat me some more. That happened during a couple of days repeatedly," she confessed. "I can tell you that he is very inventive when it comes to torturing and hurting someone," she continued in a shaky voice. In spite of her embarrassment, Darcy paled, remembering everything the man had done to her. She pressed her hands together when she felt that they shook.

"How did you manage to escape?" Nick asked her.

"He left the other night. I don't know where or why," she shrugged with indifference. Darcy didn't really care about Emmett's actions as long as they didn't involve her.

The thought that she was selfish nudged at her. However, everything that had happened to her was still vivid in her mind, and she couldn't shake the fear.

"I had already noticed that whenever Emmett went out, he took most of his men with him," Darcy continued. "I took advantage of that and sneaked out of the house at about ten at night."

"So, when I found you, you had already wandered up the mountain for a night and a day," Nick concluded without expression.

Darcy just nodded but didn't say a thing. She expected Nick to tell her to get lost at any moment now.

"All right," Nick said. "We have to think of a plan now. Emmett will be back. That's no doubt about that."

CHAPTER TWELVE

"I THINK I SHOULD CALL my mum," Darcy said. She had been waiting for several minutes for Nick to say something. But then, the man had just been pacing the kitchen, his fingers knotted at the back of his head.

"What?" Nick turned to Darcy with incredulity. Her words stumped him. "Why would you want to talk to your mother now?" Nick asked Darcy with bewilderment.

"Because she requested that I keep her posted. Of course, during the last few days, I couldn't do it," Darcy explained patiently.

"So, let me get this right. The woman threw you into Driscoll's arms, and you still want to keep her posted about what is going on," he repeated in a puzzled tone of voice. He tried to make heads and tales of Darcy's reasons, but her intentions didn't make a spit of sense to him.

"I can't think like that," Darcy shook her head stubbornly. "She hasn't always been real mother material. I know that. But I can't assume that she didn't care about me when she pushed me toward Emmett."

Nick looked at her with disbelief. He made a place for blind loyalty in his mind, but in his opinion, Darcy went way too far with that.

"All right," he accepted with resignation. Nick couldn't change Darcy's reasoning, after all. She needed to find out how things stood by herself.

"You will call her but not from here. We'll drive down the mountain. I have a phone that can't be traced, and the phone number isn't displayed. At least, we'll be safe even if she wants to tell the number to her chum, Driscoll," Nick said, standing up.

Darcy stared at him wide-eyed. She couldn't believe that the man thought so ill of her mother. Nick hadn't even met her yet to make an opinion.

"You'll see you are wrong," Darcy replied with conviction.

"Well, then, let's go and prove me wrong," Nick retorted. He reached out to her and helped her stand up.

"We're going now?" Darcy asked with astonishment, and her eyes shifted to the window.

The rain hadn't tired yet. If anything, the force of the storm had increased since Darcy and Nick returned to the house.

"But it's awful out there," she said, pointing to the window.

"I know that," Nick said, nodding in agreement. "And it will get worse. Still, I have a four-wheeler. Anyway, it's easier to go down the mountain now before the ground is saturated with water. Tomorrow, it won't be so easy," Nick explained to Darcy. "Your pants must still be wet. I have some sweatpants you can borrow," he told her.

Darcy's eyes swept over his body from the top of his head to his toes. The woman blushed in the process and dipped her head. After a couple of seconds, she looked at her body with a meaningful look. She tilted her head and lifted her left brow.

"I don't think it will work," she informed him in a flippant tone of voice. "If you haven't noticed, you're at least one foot taller than I," she pointed out.

Nick's lips twitched. First, he rubbed his hands off his pants and then his chin. Darcy's purpose hadn't been to call his attention upon her small frame, or the curves barely covered. The t-shirt had dipped lower and exposed half her breasts by now. However, the result was the same. "I know that you are smaller than I," Nick replied after he repressed his hilarity. "You can roll up the sweatpants. Anyway, it's not like you had any other option. You're the one who wants to tell your mother what happened, not me," he chid to her.

At first, Darcy's eyes narrowed dangerously. After a few seconds of silence, she replied, "All right, I will borrow those sweatpants from you. Do you want to leave now?" Darcy asked, walking by him and holding her head high.

"That's what I thought," Nick nodded.

However, Darcy couldn't see him. She had already walked past him and reached the kitchen door.

"It will be much worse later, I told you," Nick repeated. He followed the woman but in a less quick step. The man was more interested in the subtle balance of Darcy's hips and the enticing moves of her backside.

"All right, then," Darcy replied, and suddenly turned to Nick.

Nick winced when she surprised him appraising her charms, but it was too late to do anything about it. If he had kept his wits about him, he might have sensed that Darcy intended to turn back to him.

Darcy's mouth became a thin line, and she braced her hands on her hips. She couldn't believe her eyes. The woman hadn't thought that Nick would pry on her. Not after she told him about what Emmett had done to her.

Nick put up his hands to warn the rage he could read in Darcy's eyes.

"I didn't intend any disrespect. I'm a man, though, and I have eyes. Of course, I will look. But you should know that I can watch without touching, so you don't have to worry about that. Some men don't attack women," Nick attempted to calm the fury and reproaches he could see on Darcy's face. "I can imagine that you wouldn't welcome any man's advances right now, and I won't make any. You are a guest in my house, Darcy, and I respect that. Besides, I don't defile unwilling young women," he remarked, and his tone of voice turned steely. "If a woman doesn't want me, it's no big deal. I move on."

Nick imagined that he might anger her some more with his words, but then, he hadn't thought that Darcy would compare him to Driscoll. A man could darn watch without automatically jumping a woman. Her attitude offended him.

"You will find the sweatpants in the bottom drawer on the left in my room," Nick informed her in a cold tone of voice. "I will be waiting here until you change your clothes. I don't want you to think I would throw you on my bed and have my way with you," he said bitingly.

Darcy wanted to reply and probably apologize if he read her features correctly. However, Nick decided not to give her the chance to do it.

He resented her for the moment and didn't feel like hearing any hollow excuses. Nick turned on his heel and left the kitchen before Darcy. He headed toward a small room at the back of the house.

Darcy watched the man's departure wide-eyed and felt guilty for offending him. Still, she thought that Nick should have shown more understanding of her behavior.

Darcy went out of the kitchen just in time to see Nick getting into the back room, she had seen earlier. After a quick survey, Darcy had concluded that it was Nick's study.

She hadn't lingered in that room for long. The woman had just swept the floor and dusted the surfaces in her sight. She had attempted to open the drawers and snoop into the man's life, but she had the surprise to find them locked.

At the time, Darcy regretted that she had refused Dusty, one of her father's friend's son, when he offered to teach her how to pry a lock open. Darcy hadn't realized it then, but now she knew that that would have been quite a handy skill to have.

Pensively, Darcy climbed up the stairs toward Nick's room. She had checked his bedroom as well. The man didn't keep anything of interest there, and she had been disappointed in her efforts.

CHAPTER THIRTEEN

NICK DROVE HIS JEEP down the mountain through the torrential rain, and the car often slid through the mud. Whenever that happened, Darcy feared that they would stop in one of the trees, lining the so-called road. She felt her heart in her throat and clung to the door handle with all her might.

When they left the cottage, Nick had told her that they wouldn't take the main road. He didn't put it beyond Driscoll's way of thinking to have left someone to survey the lane. Nick didn't doubt that, in the end, he and Darcy would have to confront Driscoll. However, Nick preferred to do it on his terms and at a later time.

The car drive took forever. Nick hadn't stopped until they reached the other side of the mountain, close to Shelby. He parked his car at the far end of the parking lot of one of the hotels and put out the headlights so that no one could see in the vehicle and identify the people inside. Then, he handed an untraceable cell phone to Darcy.

"Don't give your mother any specific information about your present situation. Don't tell her where you are, or that you're with me," Nick warned her in a severe tone of voice.

"I know you trust your mother, Darcy, and I can understand that. Still, wait for a while, at least until you are sure that she wouldn't divulge your whereabouts to Driscoll."

Darcy took the phone from him with a hesitant gesture. She watched Nick from under her lashes for a few seconds, and then she directed the cobalt of her eyes straight into his.

"Would you prefer that I put the phone on speaker?" she asked him.

Nick pondered her proposition, and after a few seconds, he nodded. "Yes, I think so. If anything seems untoward, then we can cut the conversation short," Nick said.

Darcy shrugged, but she believed that the man exaggerated. She thought that Nick had probably been one of those kids who liked to play spies and other things like that, and that was why he saw conspiracies everywhere.

Darcy dialed her mother's number, and her call was answered almost immediately. "Hi, mum, it's me, Darcy," she said.

"Where the heck, are you, girl?" her mother's shout burst into the car. "What came over you to leave such a fine man and put him through hell?" the woman asked Darcy with irritation. "I couldn't believe my ears when I heard that. I still can't believe that you are so selfish and irresponsible," Darcy's mother scolded her.

"He isn't a fine man, mother," Darcy replied in a huff. "He raped and beat me and..."

"Don't be stupid, girl," her mother interrupted her. "The man just backhanded you. That's no big deal. When you have such a man in your hand, you don't look at such things."

"Are you serious?" Darcy hardly pushed the words out of her mouth. Her throat constricted, and she couldn't breathe. She couldn't believe that her own mother would say such a thing.

"Of course, I am. Get back where you belong," Darcy's mother ordered her. "Where are you by the way?" the woman asked with suspicion.

Darcy looked at Nick but couldn't read anything on his face. She lifted her brows, asking him what to do. Nick just shrugged. He didn't give her any indication about what she should do.

"Darcy, tell me where you are, and right this moment. Emmett will forgive you if you get back to him now. If you prevaricate, he will wash his hands off you, and with that, my chances to get what I deserve will also go down the toilet," her mother practically yelled.

"I won't ever return to Emmett, mother," Darcy replied in a quiet tone of voice, and she shook her head as if her mother could see her.

"You, ungrateful child," her mother scolded her in an angry tone of voice. "Tell me where you are, and I'll come to talk some sense into you. You don't think clearly right now, and it's evident that you don't know what is good for you," the woman added in a sarcastic tone of voice.

"You've always been too stupid for your sake. And I've always had to come and get you out of trouble," she also thought to mention. "Now, tell me where to come for you," the woman ordered in an authoritative tone of voice.

Darcy just shook her head once more, and tears welled in her eyes. She tried not to let them fall, but she failed.

Until then, Nick had listened to the entire exchange without a word or showing what he thought. Now he took the phone from Darcy's trembling fingers gently. He shook his head with regret and disconnected the call.

The man placed the phone back into the glove compartment and stared out of the windshield for a few moments. He seemed to make up his mind about something. When he turned back toward Darcy, the resolution on Nick's face took her breath away.

He just slid his arm around her shoulder and pulled her to him. Nick encircled Darcy tightly in his arms and rubbed her tense back with his right hand. The fingers of his left hand curved around Darcy's head and pulled it on his shoulder. He didn't say anything, just kept looking out of the window over the woman's head.

Darcy's fingers clung to Nick's shirt, and she cried quietly, ashamed of her weakness and of her mother's betrayal. She had always known that Wanda Burnett was a selfish woman, and she cared most about her well-being. However, she had hoped that Wanda cared at least a little about her only daughter.

Minutes passed, but Nick didn't rush Darcy. He let her cry until all the tension seeped out of her body, and he felt Darcy pliable and soft in his arms. Nick brushed the hair off her face, and then said in a soft voice, "Let's go home, Darcy. We'll change nothing sitting here. We have to make some plans, sweetheart."

Darcy pulled back out of Nick's arms and glanced at him from under her eyelashes. She nodded briefly and then sat back in her car seat.

PULLED IN

Nick watched her for a few more seconds. Then he leaned over her and fastened her seatbelt. Darcy's body tingled under his touch, and her face turned red.

Nick straightened and looked out of the windshield again. Then, he turned the car around and began the arduous trip back up the mountain toward his cottage.

CHAPTER FOURTEEN

THE MORNING CAME FAR too early for Darcy. The young woman had barely closed her eyes that the sun woke her up, shining over the shadows on her face. She didn't know what time it was but estimated that she had slept well after nine.

Darcy climbed off the bed and shuffled her feet to the window that overlooked the trail to the stables. She opened it to take a look outside, and the distinct clatter of hooves reached her ears.

For a second, her heart froze. She thought that Emmett had found her and came to take her back by force.

Darcy couldn't make her feet move, although her mind screamed at her to run away from the window and hide somewhere. Her fingers clung to the windowsill with so much force that her knuckles whitened.

Nick's silhouette appeared in her line of vision, mounted on a chestnut mare, and Darcy groaned. "You have to pull yourself together, girl," she admonished herself loudly.

Most of the time, Darcy lived by herself, so she didn't encounter many people. Her mother used to drag her here or there to various parties that Darcy actually detested. Otherwise, Darcy would have seen only the grooms that worked with her in the stable.

Anyway, evenings belonged to her, and the woman spent most of them alone. She preferred her own company because she could relax. That was why Darcy had got into the habit of talking to herself. However, sometimes she scolded herself for that. She was far too young for such a nasty habit.

Darcy admired Nick's posture on the horse and his muscular thighs. The man didn't use a whip on his mount, but he controlled the mare only with his legs and by pulling the reins. Being too tall and broad, Nick couldn't have made a living as a jockey. However, that didn't mean that the man wasn't a good rider. Darcy knew to make the difference between the wannabes and the real deal, and Nick was a natural.

She watched Nick for a few more minutes until he led the mare into the pen, where his horses ran free. Then Darcy left the window and moseyed to the bathroom to take care of her morning routine.

Afterward, Darcy thought of going downstairs. She needed to eat something because she hadn't eaten anything the night before in spite of Nick's attempts to persuade her to have a bite. The woman had been troubled and disappointed, but now, her appetite came back. Her belly growled, and Darcy rubbed it with her palm. "Only wait for a bit. We'll go and have a bite in a jiffy," Darcy reassured her noisy stomach.

NICK HAD FELT DARCY'S eyes on him when he returned with Augusta from their regular ride. However, he didn't give any sign that he had noticed her interest.

The man also sensed the moment Darcy left the window and chanced a look toward her bedroom. As expected, she wasn't there anymore.

Nick had noticed that her strength was depleted, and she was upset the night before, so he had thought to let her sleep a little longer that morning. She definitely needed to rest. Although Nick hadn't believed that Darcy would stay in bed until noon, he didn't mind that. Quite the opposite. The man hadn't wanted her to witness his efforts to secure the perimeter.

Right after Emmett Driscoll had moved into the area, Nick found out about his maneuvers to grab all available land from the people in the neighboring counties.

Nick had decided then that proofing his ranch against unwanted attacks was in order. At the time, Nick had set up several devices to survey the comings and goings on his land. He didn't want to be taken by surprise. However, he had decided against using all the sensors. Most were just in place for the future.

Now, Nick considered that that future arrived. Therefore, he woke up at four in the morning to take care of everything, although he hadn't rested too much during the last two nights because of Darcy's bitter crying.

Nick had spent about three hours making the tour of a part of his property. The man had already secured the other three corners of his grounds along the time. He had left that side unprotected because he hadn't believed that Driscoll would come that way. And still, Darcy had arrived from that direction. Nick didn't know about her presence on his land until she had reached the ranch house.

Nick didn't want to have such surprises again, so he had gone out early in the morning to activate his security devices. Now the man was sure that he had the ranch covered from all directions.

Nick had connected all his motion sensors to a small tablet that he kept on himself in a pouch tied to his waist under the shirt. If a sensor had been activated, a pitched sound would have warned him about a breach in the territory.

The man knew that he had to up his game a bit, so he had also decided to install some defense measures during that day and the following days. He hadn't just had the time for that yet.

Nonetheless, Nick also needed to take care of his horses. He had three more horses to train that morning, and for the first time in his life, he was torn between his duty and a woman.

Nick wanted to be in the cottage when Darcy would come downstairs. He had thought of making some fresh coffee for her. Nick couldn't explain to himself why he felt such an urge to serve her but couldn't suppress his wish. Mumbling, Nick called himself a fool repeatedly.

Still, the man put the saddle he had just taken off the mare on the fence. He slapped the horse on her flank to make her go to her mates and then strode toward the cottage. He decided to ride the other three mounts later.

Darcy was nowhere in sight when Nick entered the kitchen. The noise of water crossing through the old plumbing announced him that Darcy was still in the shower.

Satisfied, the man rushed to the stove and took the coffee pot to throw away the coffee he had made that morning. Then, he quickly cleaned the kettle to make fresh coffee.

Nick measured ground coffee and water in the pot and put it to boil on the stove. He looked around and thought of making some bacon and eggs. Nick remembered well that Darcy had told him that she didn't know how to cook, and he thought with amusement that the two of them were two peas in a pod. With a shrug, the man started on the omelet, resigned to the thought that they wouldn't eat too well around there. After all, food wasn't everything.

Nick had finished with everything when Darcy stepped into the kitchen. The man had already poured the coffee into the mugs and set two plates filled with bacon and eggs on the table.

Shyly, Darcy stopped in her track. Nick turned toward her and waved his hand, inviting her to come to the table and eat.

"You shouldn't have left your work," Darcy told him while sitting down. "I might not know much about cooking, but I'm able to make an omelet," she smiled at him.

Nick just shrugged with indifference and sipped from his coffee. "I was hungry anyway," he said. "I'd have made some for me, so it isn't a big deal."

Darcy forked some eggs and shoved them into her mouth. She noticed that Nick wanted to play casual, so she decided not to insist on that line of discussion anymore.

"Are you going back to the horses after you finish eating?" she asked, glancing at Nick from under her lashes.

Nick just nodded. Busy cleaning off his plate, the man didn't want to talk right then. He had already worked a sweat that morning and was starving.

Darcy sighed inaudibly and continued to eat in silence. She thought that Nick had reasons to feel like brooding and didn't want to upset him more.

Once finished with his food, Nick took his plate to the sink, and Darcy's gaze followed him. The man turned to her, crossing his arms over his chest. Darcy searched Nick's eyes but didn't read anything in his pupils. However, his stance showed that he wanted to keep her at a distance, and anxiety weighed on her chest.

"What do you want to do when you have finished eating?" Nick asked her suddenly.

Darcy didn't expect him to talk, so his words startled her. "Do you want me to leave?" Darcy asked Nick in a small voice. It wasn't as if Darcy didn't expect him to tell her to go.

Nick frowned and scowled at her. "Why would you think that? Don't be stupid. Of course, I don't want you to leave," the man snapped at her. "I was just asking if you had plans for the day. If not, you can come with me for a ride," he explained in a surly tone of voice.

CHAPTER FIFTEEN

"I KNOW THAT MR. DRISCOLL asked around about a black-haired, blue-eyed woman," Bill said, leaning over the counter of the bar.

The skinny man watched Frank sideways with expecting eyes for a few moments. Then Bill turned his head and spat the tobacco he had been chewing all afternoon.

Frank turned to Bill with reticence. Everybody in the little town knew Bill, and most of the people despised and feared him.

The man was good at ferreting out the worst gossip around and selling the information to the highest bidder. Bill wouldn't give anything for free, and his prices for tale-telling went quite high.

Frank moved his glance to his mate and frowned. Gabe didn't pay any attention to the word exchange that went between Frank and Bill. Gabe was intently watching a redhead.

The woman was rolling her hips, dancing alone in front of the jukebox, she had just fed with coins. Gabe's eyes had zeroed in on her behind, and his pupils had slightly dilated.

Frank elbowed Gabe in his ribs with disgust to make him pay attention. Gabe groaned and returned Frank the honor without pity.

Frank rubbed his midriff, where Gabe's elbow caught him, and his eyes turned hard. Then the man tilted his head toward Bill. Gabe understood that Frank meant business, so he leaned back and measured the middle-aged man with contemptuous eyes.

Over six feet tall, half-Scandinavian and half-Cherokee, Gabe cut an impressive figure. Chickenpox had scarred the man's face in his childhood, and his face looked harsher.

Few people could look straight at Gabe. Most shifted their eyes to the side or downward. A very well-directed fist had crooked Gabe's bulbous nose when he was in his teens. In revenge, Gabe had broken his attacker's arms. After that episode, people feared him and avoided any direct confrontation with the giant.

When Gabe aimed his cold eyes at someone, people would scurry away or shudder, and Bill didn't make an exception. His legs turned weak immediately, and he needed to cling to the counter with all his might not to turn into a puddle on the floor.

"You say you have information about the broad," Gabe drawled, staring the man down.

Bill swallowed hard and nodded. To find his voice was out of the question.

"Hmm, I see," Gabe mumbled his displeasure and scowled at the man. Gabe liked getting the information but despised the snitches. He picked up his longneck beer bottle off the counter with measured gestures and gulped a mouthful. When he took the bottle from his mouth, Gabe wiped off his lips with his sleeve.

Frank knew Gabe well and didn't intervene. He waited patiently to see what his mate had in mind.

Gabe left the bottle on the wooden counter of the bar, and again, he turned his eyes in the direction of the redhead he was watching earlier. The man smacked his lips noisily and suddenly stood up. He started going toward the woman but stopped only after three steps. He didn't bother to turn his head to Bill but said, "You'll tell everything to Frank. He'll give you a twenty, not more."

Then Gabe lengthened his strides, and in a few seconds, he reached the woman, who was still rolling her hips in front of the jukebox.

Gabe slid one arm around her waist and pulled her forcefully to him. The woman huffed when her back met the man's firm body and then twittered on embarrassed laughter. The woman didn't even dream of refusing Gabe's advances. The man's presence frightened and aroused her at the same time. She turned around in his arms and draped her body around Gabe's.

Wide-eyed, Bill watched the couple's interactions a few seconds, and a pang of envy fluttered in his chest. Women never reacted to him that way. Afterward, the man turned to Frank. "Do we have a deal?" Bill asked boldly.

Gabe's departure had brought his self-confidence back. He was ready to talk business now, and Frank didn't scare him at all.

Frank scowled, and his upper lip bared his teeth. His sharp incisors shone in the light coming from above his head. The man searched his pocket, took out a crumpled banknote, and threw it on the counter with irritation. "Now, talk," Frank barked.

Immediately, Bill fished the banknote with two fingers and licked his lips with satisfaction. He waved to the barman with impatience. "Give me a longneck, Jim," Bill shouted and laid the crumpled banknote on the counter, tapping his finger onto the scarred top of the bar counter.

Bill finally started talking when Frank's patience had already reached the end of its rope. The man was about to grab the weasel and shake him.

Fury darkened Frank's face at Bill's words, and a metallic glint shone in the man's eyes. He clenched his teeth together and signaled Gabe to leave the broad and return to the bar counter.

However, Gabe shook his head in denial. Right then, he was busy charming the redhead and couldn't care less about what Bill had said. The man pulled the woman closer to him and continued swaying in his own rhythm.

He knew that he would score that night, and he always enjoyed his encounters with that broad. Gabe didn't see the point in letting the opportunity pass by him.

Frank gnashed his teeth in frustration and ordered another beer. He knew he couldn't rush his friend. Gabe functioned only on his own schedule. He didn't care about other people or urgent matters.

PULLED IN

On the one hand, Frank couldn't wait to tell everything he had found out to Driscoll, yet, on the other, he dreaded to face the man alone. Driscoll's rages were memorable.

Frank had already made Emmett Driscoll's probation list, and he feared the man's reaction to his words.

Emmett Driscoll hated to be taken for a sucker. This time, he had been made a fool and a big time.

CHAPTER SIXTEEN

THE MEN CRINGED WHEN Driscoll's roar reached them. Frank and Gabe had decided to speak to their boss alone, and they had left their teams in the ranch yard with orders to wait for them.

Dean, too young and stupid to understand what was really going on, grinned widely. Ben, Frank's right hand, thwacked him over the head.

"Are you out of your mind, kiddo?" Ben asked the young man, and his eyebrows bunched on his forehead. "When the big boss is angry, you don't grin, stupid boy," he advised Dean in a hard tone of voice.

Dean hung his head in shame and shuffled to get behind the others. The boy didn't understand why he was always in the wrong. Eager to please, he would make mistakes all the time.

"We'll erase him and his ranch off the face of the earth," Driscoll shouted at the tops of his lungs. "And the broad will pay dearly for everything."

Frank's story had inflamed Driscoll's rage. His inability to find Darcy had already angered him before his men came back to him with what Bill told them.

In general, Emmett Driscoll could keep his cool somewhat and rarely had outbursts of rage, but now, he couldn't control himself. He couldn't bear to know that Nick had lied him to his face and in front of the broad.

Surely, Darcy had been there when Nick told Driscoll that he hadn't seen her.

Driscoll poured himself a large helping of bourbon and tossed it to the back of his throat. The bite of the alcohol made him hiss, and then he threw the glass into the opposite wall.

The noise of broken glass reached the yard, and most of the men huddled there exchanged meaningful looks. They looked scared but ready to carry out the boss's orders.

Six men had grouped aside from the others, though. Just invited to join Emmett Driscoll's advanced teams, they welcomed that invitation with dread, and their faces wrinkled with concern. They glanced at each other, and their gazes expressed the same thing. They didn't think that they should have been there with the others in the yard and witnessed that discussion.

Rumors had reached their ears about some of Driscoll's deals. However, until then, they had never participated actively in the principal part of Driscoll's business. They usually guarded the stables and the ranch. When Driscoll was in dire need of people, they were also ordered to take care of moving or securing the children and women Driscoll was trafficking.

They had heard that some people met their maker as a result of Driscoll's orders, inclusively a few from Driscoll's teams. However, the six men had never been directly involved in a murder. They had wallowed in the illusory safety given by their distancing from some of Driscoll's activities. Now, their confidence shook.

It seemed that they had just made Driscoll's attack teams, and most of the men in those teams didn't enjoy a long life. A lot of them had disappeared when Driscoll was dissatisfied with the outcome of an action. Emmett Driscoll had spared only Gabe and Frank, but then, the two men were Driscoll's right and left hands.

Their features darkened, Frank and Gabe came out of the ranch house with purposeful strides. Gabe's eyes shone dangerously, and Frank's left eyelid twitched involuntarily.

Waving his hand, Gabe called to the people in the yard to gather around him and then told them, "I want you to wait in your barracks. No one is on leave starting now. Frank and I have to make some plans, and then we will give you your orders."

One of the six people, who had remained somewhat to the side, stepped forward. He was a younger man, around twenty-three. The wind had tousled his dark hair, and the man looked like an unmade bed. He shoved his hands into his pockets so that Gabe wouldn't see that he shook, and he tried to assume an assertive stance.

Behind the young man, Ben shook his head. He thought that it was a pity, but the guy wouldn't have a long life.

"Do we have to wait, too?" the young man asked.

Gabe's slanted eyes thundered at the man, and his mouth became a thin line. He didn't answer immediately. Gabe knew that the young man's apprehension would increase if he had to wait for a reply, and he milked that strategy to the maximum.

"Why would you be here if you weren't involved in the active teams, Darren?" Gabe barked and took a menacing step toward the man. "I can fire you right now," Gabe continued in a harsh tone of voice.

Darren shook his head immediately. He didn't know for sure what happened, but he had never seen or heard anything of the people that Gabe fired. Darren didn't want to join their ranks.

His lips taut over his teeth, Gabe grinned with satisfaction. He had known that Darren would step back if he threatened him. Besides, Gabe enjoyed seeing people shuddering before him.

CHAPTER SEVENTEEN

NICK WOKE UP WITH A startle, and his nose twitched. He smelled the smoke and swore viciously. He understood that at least one of his motion sensor devices had malfunctioned, and now he had unwanted guests in the house. Nick should have checked all the sensors instead of one out of three. *'You're slipping, man, exactly when you shouldn't,'* Nick said under his breath.

In fact, afraid for Darcy's safety, Nick hurried to come back to the ranch house and hadn't tested all the devices. He hadn't wanted to leave the woman alone for too long time. Driscoll might have come back at any moment. Darcy had been sleeping at the time, and anyone could have captured her by surprise.

Nick jumped out of bed and pulled on some sweatpants with swift moves. However, he didn't bother with footwear or a shirt. The man suspected that the home invaders had deactivated the fire alarms. Otherwise, their sound would have warned him about the smoke sooner.

Nick opened a drawer, took out a small towel, and soaked it with half of the water in the jar he kept next to the bed on the night table. The man wanted to be ready in case the smoke behind his door was so dense that he couldn't breathe.

Nick took care to grab the semiautomatic pistol he hid under his pillow every night and ran out of the room quietly. Noises came from downstairs, but Nick was sure that no one had got upstairs yet. He would have heard their steps, regardless of how tired he would have been.

The man reached Darcy's room with a few giant strides. He was frantically thinking about how to wake her up so that Darcy wouldn't get scared and scream.

Nick didn't want to lose the element of surprise and let the people who ransacked the rooms downstairs know that he was awake.

When Darcy's door opened silently, Nick sighed with relief. The moon shone through the window at the end of the hallway. Darcy could see that Nick was coming toward her and didn't get spooked.

Nick's gaze met Darcy's, and the man understood that the woman was terrified. He put a finger to his lips to let her know that she should keep quiet. Then the man grabbed Darcy's hand and pulled her after him toward his bedroom. Darcy's eyes widened, but she didn't resist and followed him.

Once inside the room, Nick closed the door silently behind them and led Darcy toward the massive wardrobe that covered the entire western wall of the room.

Darcy had wondered about the size of that piece of furniture in the morning, mainly because it was mostly empty. She had looked inside and found just a bunch of shirts and two pairs of jeans.

PULLED IN

Nick opened one of the side doors, stepped inside the wardrobe, and pulled Darcy in his wake. Inside now, the man pressed his hand onto a discolored spot on the wooden plank at the back. Under Darcy's stunned eyes, the board slid away with a hiss and opened toward a winded and steep staircase.

Nick made a sign to Darcy to stay put and waited to see her nod of acceptance. Their eyes had already accustomed to the shadows. Then Nick hurried back into the room and pulled a shirt on. He reflected for a second and also grabbed a pair of sneakers. Nick didn't know where he would have to go after seeing Darcy to safety, so he thought that he should be prepared for everything. Darcy wondered at the man's speed of getting dressed.

Once he finished with that, Nick opened one of the drawers of his small chest of drawers and took out another small towel for Darcy. He poured on it all the water left in the jar on his nightstand.

Afterward, Nick grabbed two flashlights he kept in the drawer of the night table. He returned into the wardrobe with quick steps and lit one of the torches at the same time.

Nick shut the wardrobe door behind him and waved to Darcy to move. They got out of the closet and onto the top step, and the man pulled a lever. The panel slid back into place noiselessly.

Nick leaned over Darcy and whispered to her to start climbing down behind him. "Hold on the back of my shirt," Nick advised her in a quiet tone of voice. "If anything, just tug, and I will stop," he promised.

Darcy didn't know the place, and the steps were narrow, so they needed a few minutes to reach the bottom of the staircase. The woman slid a couple of times, and Nick had to grab her so that she wouldn't go down hard. Nick knew that he would have gone down with her, as well.

The stairs led to a fork in a long dark corridor. Darcy tried to find her bearings, but she didn't really know where they were.

"We're just behind the cellar," Nick explained to her, understanding why she looked around with apprehension. "This corridor will lead you to shelter, behind the barn," Nick showed to the right. No one will find you there," he reassured Darcy.

Nick lit the second flashlight and handed it to the woman. Then, he squeezed her shoulder for reassurance, and with a sign of his head, he encouraged her to move.

Darcy nodded and started ahead. After a few steps, she realized that Nick didn't follow her, so she stopped and turned her head to him, just in time to notice that Nick had just taken the other way.

"What are you doing?" Darcy whispered furiously. "Aren't you coming with me?"

Nick returned quickly to Darcy and put his finger on her mouth. "Shush, we don't need to announce them that we're down here," he whispered close to Darcy's ear.

"Aren't you coming with me?" Darcy asked again, quietly this time.

"I can't come with you," Nick shook his head. "But you'll be fine there. The place is set up with everything you need for an entire week if necessary."

"But what about you? Where are you going? What are you going to do?" Anxiety got the best of her, and Darcy's questions tumbled one after another.

Nicks suppressed his laughter and shook his head again. "I need to take the vermin out," Nick replied quietly to her. "When I finish, I'll come and get you," he promised again.

Darcy searched Nick's features attentively to see if he lied to her. She didn't notice anything else but the resolution in his eyes and the firm line of his mouth. The woman wrinkled her nose. She didn't like it that he left her alone, and at the same time, she was afraid of what might happen to him.

"They are so many," Darcy whispered in dismay. "Emmett would have come with a lot of them. How can you fight against so many men?" she wondered.

"I have skills," Nick replied in a dry tone of voice. "Don't think about what I have to do. You just go where I told you. If I don't have to worry about you, I'll be fine," he nudged her to go.

"Just promise me that you won't move from the shelter until I come after you," Nick insisted.

Darcy nodded with hesitation. She had already decided to stop nagging him. Nick needed to be calm if he intended to put up a fight against so many men.

The woman raised her hands to Nick's shoulders, and under the man's surprised eyes, she rose on tiptoes, and her lips brushed off his mouth with a featherlike touch. Then she drew back and looked straight into Nick's coffee eyes. The man glanced back at her, and a strange light danced in his pupils. Darcy stroked the side of Nick's face and then hurried down the corridor.

CHAPTER EIGHTEEN

SOMEONE HAD SEARCHED the cellar carefully, and signs of several people trespassing Nick's basement abounded everywhere. Nick kept about ten sacks of grain in there. Someone had cleaved all of them and spread the grains on the granite floor. Nick's eyes narrowed to slits when the man noticed the waste. He needed those grains for his stud.

The vandals had also started fires in three places, using gasoline as an accelerator, and timed the blaze. They probably wanted to have time to search around the rest of the house as well.

The perpetrators hadn't discovered Nick's secret entrance before they abandoned the cellar. They had just moved to other areas of the house.

Nick put the fires out once he had reached the cellar. The man had had the foresight to place a couple of fire extinguishers in the secret corridor right near the entrance in the basement. He had learned to plan for any situation, after all.

Now Nick hunched underneath the basement door leading to the exterior and listened attentively. Rushed steps passed by, and Nick estimated that they moved in the direction of the barn behind the house. Although he was itching to take action, Nick forced himself to wait patiently for a few more minutes, and only then, he unlocked the latch.

Nick cracked the door open and looked outside. The way seemed free. The man sneaked out quietly and climbed the steps with catlike moves. The giant squatted in the shadow of the building and waited for a few more seconds.

A man of action, Nick loathed waiting. Nevertheless, waiting had kept him breathing in various circumstances along the time, so he resigned to waiting now, as well.

The night sky was clear. The moon shone over the open area behind the ranch house. Nobody prowled around there. Suddenly, steps sounded close to his position, and Nick sharpened his ears. The man judged that two people came from around the corner, so he stood up carefully, always keeping to the shadows, and lowered the cellar door with one hand. Nick noted with satisfaction that it didn't squeak and congratulated himself for having oiled it.

Nick tiptoed to the corner of the building and leaned on it. He drew a quiet breath and tilted his head around the corner for a better view of the two men who argued in hushed tones.

Nick put a name on the younger one immediately. He remembered that Darcy had described the men who looked for her. She had told him that the boy's name was Dean.

Nick had seen the other man down in town a couple of times and remembered him well. Nick had wondered about the company the guy kept. He didn't seem to fit in with Driscoll's hoards. The man was quiet and didn't get involved in quarrels like Driscoll's other men did.

PULLED IN

"Don't be stupid, Dean," Darren hissed. "Driscoll is furious. He's out of his mind right now because he couldn't find anyone inside the house. No one came out either, although he set fires inside the building. Haven't you seen Gabe's eyes? Someone will have to pay for this disaster, and I won't be the scapegoat. Come with me, you, stupid kid," Darren begged Dean, afraid about what might happen to the boy. He didn't put it beyond Gabe to take his revenge on the young man.

Dean shook his head furiously. He shoved Darren with both hands but didn't have the strength to throw the man to the ground.

"You're a coward, Darren. I will tell on you, you'll see," the boy chanted in a pitched tone of voice.

Darren stumbled but held his position. He shook his head with regret.

The boy's IQ laid around seventy, and Darren knew that he wouldn't be able to make Dean believe anything. The boy idolized Gabe, and he wouldn't have done anything else but what Driscoll's right hand said.

"You can tell on me if you like," Darren shrugged with disinterest. "I'm out of here anyway. I don't want to go to jail for arson and murder," he replied with nonchalance. "I haven't signed up for that."

Darren turned his back to the boy and headed to the forest, where they had left their horses earlier. He thought of riding out of the area and sending the mount to Driscoll afterward. He wouldn't have dared to steal the man's horse.

Dean took out the knife he carried in a sheath at his belt, and with a cry, he jumped Darren from behind. Nick rushed forward to stop him, but the boy still had the time to shove the knife into Darren's back.

Darren fell with a woof on the grassy ground, and Dean raised the knife for another blow. However, steely fingers laced to the boy's wrist.

"Let it go, boy," Nick advised him in a quiet but menacing tone of voice.

Dean's eyes widened. He needed a couple of seconds to recover, and then he started screaming from the top of his lungs, "He's here. He's here."

With his other hand, Dean tried to push Nick, but the man was ready for the kid. A well-placed fist in Dean's temple rendered the boy an unmoving heap on the ground. Nick hadn't released Dean's wrist before he punched the boy, so the bones shattered with a sickening sound, and Dean's fingers dropped the knife. The boy just groaned before losing consciousness.

Nick watched the boy for a couple of seconds to make sure that he didn't move anymore. With a swift move, the man unbuckled the boy's belt and tied his legs tightly. When he finished with that, he unlaced one of Dean's boots and used the lace to bind the young man's hands together at his back.

The man knew that the boy wouldn't be able to use his right hand for the moment. However, Dean could have used his left to untie his legs, and Nick didn't want him to move.

When he had Dean trussed safely, Nick picked him up and carried him to the entrance to the basement.

He opened the door and climbed down the first three steps. From there, Nick threw Dean inside, without any care for the boy's well-being. The guy could turn black and blue for all that Nick cared.

The man returned to Darren, who was still lying where he had fallen. The man panted, a sign that his wound pained him. Nick looked at the blood sipping from the injury and concluded that the boy didn't touch anything vital. Then he turned Darren on his back.

The man blinked as if he couldn't believe that he had Nick before his eyes. Fear widened his pupils, and his lips parted. Nick noticed that the man's tears had left dirty traces on his face, and he shook his head.

"Well, you're still alive," Nick remarked dryly and shrugged with indifference. "I can't take care of you right now. I've got to take care of a few more people inside the house and probably the stables," he observed.

"They haven't gotten to the stables yet," Darren whispered and licked his lips.

"That's good to know," Nick nodded. "How many people are in the house?" he asked. The young man didn't seem as bloodthirsty as his mates, so Nick thought that Darren might tell him the truth.

"Ten more people, including Driscoll, Frank, and Gabe," Darren replied. "They'll come out soon," he warned Nick. "They were about to finish when I sneaked out. The kid just followed me here. He can't believe that anyone would betray Gabe."

"Yeah, I noticed," Nick said in the same dry tone of voice. "I'll carry you into the basement for the moment. You'll survive, so don't worry. Your wound isn't deep. I think the knife didn't penetrate deeper than your muscle."

"You can't think of going after all of them by yourself," the man exclaimed with astonishment. "You won't get out of the house alive," he pointed out.

"Don't worry about me, man," Nick grinned, and his teeth shone wolfishly in the light of the moon.

Darren shuddered but refrained from saying anything more. Now, he wondered how others would fare with Nick. With Gabe's exception, all of Driscoll's men were shorter and weaker than the giant Darren had under his eyes. Their only advantage laid in their number.

Nick grabbed Darren from under the arms. He lifted Darren up and then supported him to walk to the cellar, and then down on the steep steps.

Then he led Darren to a corner that hadn't been licked by the fire and helped the man to lie down on a sack.

Nick made sure that the man would be fine and then ran to the large cupboard that lined one of the walls of the basement. Driscoll's men had pried it open, but they didn't know that he had built a secret compartment, so they had only rummaged through his tools.

Nick pressed his palm onto a spot in the upper right corner, and a panel moved to the side silently, revealing rows of guns, Tasers, and hand grenades. Beneath those, Nick had stocked a few pairs of handcuffs, hunting knives, and even a nunchuck. Two rifles hung from the back panel. Nick chose a pair of sturdy handcuffs and returned to Darren.

"Sorry, big guy," he said with a negligent shrug. "You seem an honest guy, but I trust only a few people in this world, and you're not one of them. You'll stay put until I come back for you," Nick explained and handcuffed Darren to the pipe that ran through that corner of the basement and led toward the central part of the house. Darren said nothing. The man had lost his tongue the moment he had spotted Nick's arsenal, and now Darren wondered who the man was. He just hoped that Nick wasn't one of the whackos with the army for freedom and shuddered in apprehension at that thought.

Darren didn't move a muscle while Nick handcuffed him. He didn't have the strength to do anything, and anyway, he didn't see the point to try it.

Satisfied with his handiwork, Nick stood and braced his hands on his hips. He looked at Darren and shook his head. *'What a waste,'* he thought. Then, Nick strode purposefully to his concealed cupboard and picked two angry-looking knives. He balanced them in his hand, and satisfied, he shoved them into his belt. Nick also armed himself with two semi-automatic pistols and two Tasers of the last generation.

Darren watched him wide-eyed. The man was a damn walking arsenal.

Nick surveyed the remaining weapons and shook his head. He didn't think that he needed the rifles or grenades inside the house, so he shut the board back.

The man hesitated a few moments but thought better and reopened the panel. He took a few pairs of handcuffs and hung them to his belt. Only afterward, he sealed his hide-out again.

The man turned to Dean first and looked at him. The boy was still out. Nick tore two strips from the boy's shirt and made a ball from one and shoved it into the kid's mouth. He tied the second over his mouth. Finished with Dean, he strode to Darren.

"I won't make a sound," the man promised. His lips quivered, and he licked them agitated.

Nick didn't seem to believe him, so Darren pleaded again. "I won't make a noise. I'd be in trouble, believe me. Dean would tell Gabe that I wanted to run. I promise I won't make a sound," he pleaded.

Nick tilted his head, reflecting on the man's words, and then, he nodded briefly. "I won't cover your mouth. But don't think you'd escape my wrath if you lied to me."

Darren shook his head vehemently, and Nick turned around, waving his hand with disgust. He latched the exterior door of the cellar and crossed the basement toward the door leading inside the cottage.

Darren's wide eyes followed his determined strides. The young man shook his head as if he couldn't believe his eyes. The giant was going directly into the fray.

CHAPTER NINETEEN

THE DOOR OF THE CELLAR opened into the kitchen. Nick tiptoed inside the room and surveyed the disaster. Pots and dishes had been hurled to the ground, some of them smashed in the process. Flour covered every available surface. Someone had taken out the food out of the fridge, thrown it onto the floor, and left the fridge door open.

Nick's eyes narrowed dangerously, and his face shadowed. He tightened his teeth and strode to the fridge. The man pushed the door shut with an angry move. Nick's blood hummed in his veins, and he was livid.

With angry steps, Nick turned to the kitchen door to get to the hall and avoided the pots and dishes on the floor carefully. He didn't intend to make the attackers' job easier and broadcast his arrival. He counted on surprise.

Nick stopped for a second before reaching the door and looked around again. He didn't see any signs of a fire in the kitchen and found that fact fascinating.

Voices came from the hall, so the man abandoned his train of thought. Nick couldn't make out the words, but it sounded like people arguing, and he shook his head. '*This is a quarreling lot.*'

At the kitchen door, Nick leaned on the jamb and looked outside. Two men had a dispute just a few feet from him. One of them wiped the sweat off his forehead with his sleeve negligently and then spat on the floor.

Nick tightened his teeth with fury when he saw his house treated with such disrespect. Then the man glanced the other way and saw that the hallway was free.

Quietly, Nick stepped behind the two men and hit both of them with the edge of his palms. With a strangled groan, the men started dropping to the ground, but Nick caught them just in time. He let them slide to the floor and then slapped a pair of handcuffs on them, binding them together.

Nick stared at them for a few seconds. He would have liked to drag them outside the house and leave them there like yesterday's trash, but he didn't have time for that, so he shrugged and abandoned them where they were.

Nick didn't mind if they moved, but he knew that they wouldn't be able to take the cuffs off. Anyway, they wouldn't wake up before ten or even fifteen minutes, and then it would be too late to make any noise and alert the others.

Nick moved toward the salon, and on his way, he noticed the spot of another fire. It looked like the arsonist had contended the flames and kept them alive just enough to cause some smoke.

Now Nick understood why he hadn't seen any other traces of soot. Driscoll had intended to make them believe that the house was in flames. Darcy and Nick would have run downstairs right in Driscoll's hands.

Nevertheless, the timed fire in the cellar should have rendered the cottage to cinders once Driscoll and his men had walked out.

Nick's wrath grew more. Regardless of how well-timed a fire was, the risk was still high, and Driscoll had risked more lives than only two.

Nick advanced to the salon. A quick glance told him that no one was in there. The place had been ransacked, though. Someone had slashed the sofa and the armchairs, and Nick fought to keep calm. He knew it wouldn't have helped if he had got mad, and things were just things, after all.

His study was empty, as well. However, the disaster was much more extensive there. Even the desk drawers had been smashed. Yet, the men hadn't had the means to open them. The desk was made of reinforced sturdy wood, and the invaders would have needed an ax to get inside them.

Nick grinned with satisfaction and moved on. He needed to get upstairs. Apparently, everybody was there, and he wanted to join the party.

Nick shook his head in disbelief. Driscoll proved an uninspired thug and lacked the necessary strategic skills. No one with half a brain would have left only two men down there and took all the others with him to the first floor.

Anyone could have ambushed them in there. It was only a cottage after all, not a vast area where the men could spread around.

Still, Nick knew stupid people were the most dangerous, and one could never predict their reactions.

Nick knew the exact spots where the old staircase creaked, so he climbed up the stairs without noise. Before getting to the top, the man took out one Taser and one semi-automatic pistol.

Nick had had the time to think about what he was going to do. He had decided not to kill anyone, if possible. He had planned to hurt the men and render them incapable of fighting back.

Nick just wanted them gone off his land for the moment, although he knew that things wouldn't stop there. He would have to make some plans for later, but then, he needed some backup for those plans.

The county sheriff wasn't one of the Driscoll's good friends. Nevertheless, Driscoll frightened the man, and the sheriff wouldn't have taken any measures against him. He wouldn't have intervened if Nick had had to battle with Driscoll. The man would just wait to see who won and act then.

Nick shook his head in disappointment and continued on his way upstairs. Now he could make out Driscoll's furious raging.

"Where the hell, are they? How the hell, could they have gotten out?" the man bellowed.

"Maybe they jumped out of the window, boss," Gabe's calm voice intervened.

"Are you out of your freaking mind?" Driscoll shouted at his man. "Would you see the broad jumping out of the window?"

"She definitely climbed down that balcony," Frank intervened in a small voice, and Nick understood that Frank was afraid of Driscoll. The man didn't have Gabe's shrewdness.

"We should go downstairs, boss," Gabe drawled. "They're not in here, and we're wasting time arguing. We should put the house on fire and chase after them in the woods."

"Who the hell made you the boss?" Driscoll's angry voice barked.

"Just saying, boss," Gabe replied phlegmatically.

Driscoll didn't reply immediately, and apparently, everyone waited for his answer, so Nick waited too.

"All right, we'll go downstairs and pour gasoline everywhere," Driscoll decided. "You two will come back with some gasoline upstairs. I want this cottage erased completely," he ordered some of his people.

Nick rushed down the stairs and took position behind the railing. Driscoll started down first. Nick waited until the man had climbed down half the stairs and fired his Taser at full charge.

The barb hit Driscoll right in his chest, so the man screamed and began twitching. Driscoll tried to grab the railing and stop his fall but missed. The man went down the stairs like a missile. He landed with a loud thump at the foot of the stairs. And still, his body continued convulsing.

Frank ran after Driscoll intending to help him. Nick rewarded the man's efforts by shooting a barb from his Taser right in the middle of Frank's chest.

Frank shouted in agony, but he did manage to catch the railing. His triumph lasted only a couple of seconds, though. Spasms made it impossible for him to control his fingers.

Frank involuntarily let go of the balustrade, rolled down the stairs, and landed on top of Driscoll with a whack.

Four other people also ran down the stairs to see what happened to their boss. Nick knew that he had only one more shot available in that Taser, so he chose the bigger man as the intended target and pressed the release button. Luckily, the man went down and also mowed two others in his fall. Only one man remained standing, but that didn't bother Nick much.

Nick kept an eye on the huddle at the foot of the stairs. He had the other on the men who were still standing. He noticed when Gabe and another guy appeared at the top of the staircase.

Nick shoved the semi-automatic pistol into the belt. He took out the second Taser and saw Gabe move. The man wanted to get to the weapon he had at the back of his pants and spill it in Nick.

Nick amped the charge and fired a barb directly into Gabe's rib cage. The giant fell like a log. The man next to Gabe looked down at his boss with horror in his eyes. He was unable to react for a few moments.

The guy, still standing on the stairs, had run down to attack Nick. He had already reached him by then. With an eerie calm, Nick pressed the Teaser right onto the man's torso and pressed the release button.

The shock threw Nick's target back, and the man hit the wall hard. Then he slid down, his body convulsing spasmodically.

Nick replaced the Taser in his belt and brought out the semi-automatic pistols. He trained one on the huddle on the floor, and the other on Gabe and his companion upstairs. Nick knew that men's seizures would stop soon.

Nick spoke for the first time since he shot the first barb, but groans and grumbles filled the hall, so he had to shout to be heard.

"I can fire these guns in my sleep without missing my target," he announced in a hard tone of voice.

Several pairs of eyes, filled with pain and hatred, lifted at him suddenly. All the groans and grumbling ceased, and the silence stretched for a few seconds. Nick merely bad-mugged the lot of them. He didn't care about their discomfort, and they deserved all the pain, anyway.

"I've played nice so far. In a way, you're still able to function somewhat. Let's be smart and keep it that way," Nick invited them in a dry tone of voice. "Yes, you can jump me. That is true. But I will shoot Driscoll first and Gabe second, and remember, I shoot to kill. So, think well," he warned them.

Driscoll looked straight into Nick's gaze and didn't read any hesitation in the man's impenetrable eyes. Determined to carry out his threats, Nick would kill without qualms.

Driscoll looked around. All his men had pistols, but most of them still twitched. They would have missed the target if they had fired their guns and would have likely shot each other, so Emmett Driscoll decided to hand the victory to Nick for the moment. That left a bitter taste in his mouth, and he swore to avenge his defeat. Nick would pay dearly.

Driscoll signaled his men to follow him outside and headed to the front door. His legs shook, and his fingers still convulsed. A grimace crossed his face every time latent spasms seized his muscles.

Patiently, Nick waited until Gabe climbed down the stairs with the help of his man. Gabe reached the bottom of the stairs and threw a black look at Nick.

"You'll die by my hand. Slowly and painfully," Gabe growled, and his angry eyes pierced Nick.

"Until then, don't forget to take the garbage out with you," Nick replied with nonchalance. "Two of your people are back there," he pointed to the place where he had left the men he handcuffed earlier.

With a curt sign of his head, Gabe sent his man to pick up the two left behind near the kitchen. Then Gabe leaned on the jamb of the front door and waited on the threshold for his men to return. In the meantime, he stared Nick down, but the man merely looked back at him with utter indifference.

When everyone got out of his cottage, Nick came to the front door. He gazed after the group of people that headed toward the border of the forest. Nick thought that they had left their horses there.

"Leave a horse behind," Nick shouted. "I've got another of your men here. I will drape him over the horse and send it to you."

With disgust, Driscoll just waved his hand in acknowledgment and dragged his feet toward the horses tethered in the woods. The man had never felt such intense hatred before. It ate at him, and he practically ground his teeth to powder.

The others followed after him. No one dared to say a word. Their hearts cringed when they thought of what Driscoll would do when they reached his ranch. Definitely, some of them would pay for that fiasco.

Nick kept his eyes on the men until they reached the skirt of the forest. He waited for two more minutes until a man slapped the flank of a gelding and drove the horse toward the cottage.

Nick grinned, and his lips bared his teeth. He waited until the horse got closer to him and then stepped toward the mount. The man caught the reins and led the gelding to the porch, where he tethered him to the railing.

Nick leaned on one of the pillars of the veranda, waiting with his semi-automatic pistols at the ready. The sound of hooves got lost in the forest soon. However, Nick still remained there for a few more minutes until he judged that no one would come back for him.

Only then, Nick went inside the house and locked the door behind him.

It wouldn't have helped much if anyone had wanted to get into the cottage, but at least, the sound of the door broken down would have warned Nick that he was under attack.

Nick strode to the kitchen with two purposes in mind. He needed to recharge the Tasers and had to get rid of Dean as soon as possible.

He let the Tasers recharge and headed for the cellar. The man had just reached the top of the stairs leading to the basement when the dispute between Darren and Dean reached his ears. Apparently, Dean had managed to get rid of his makeshift gag, and Nick appreciated the guy's determination.

"Gabe will slice you thin," Dean shouted, and his anger reverberated in the room.

"I don't intend to ever lay my eyes on him, so the point is moot," Darren replied calmly.

However, Nick discerned the discomfort in the man's voice. The stabbing might not have been severe, but it was painful. Darren's position on the sack didn't help him either, but Nick couldn't have let the man free to roam wherever he wanted.

"He'll find you," Dean insisted. "You'll see. You can't hide from him. You're a traitor, and you deserve to die."

"If you say so," Darren said in a soft tone of voice. "But I don't see how killing other people before getting myself killed would save me. Gabe would still kill me one day. I won't dirty my hands with innocent people's blood."

"Huh, you think you're smarter than me," Dean started to retort, but Nick had had enough and decided to stop the bickering.

"Okay, kids, the recess is over," his hard voice cut in.

"You're alive," Dean shouted with astonishment, and his eyes widened. "You can't be," the boy frowned, and confusion darkened his face.

He didn't seem to understand how it was possible. Dean had expected Gabe to come and take him from the cellar. He thought that his boss had already annihilated Nick.

"Well, I am. And now's the time for you to say goodbye. Your mount is waiting for you outside," Nick replied dryly.

He grabbed the young man's handcuffed hands and pulled him up. Nick threw Dean over the shoulder with a thump, ignoring the boy's desperate screams of pain. Before starting up the stairs, Nick turned to Darren.

"What about you? Do you want to stay or go?"

"I don't know where to go right now," the young man admitted morosely. "I haven't thought so far ahead."

PULLED IN

"Well, we'll see," Nick replied and climbed up the stairs, carrying Dean, who began shouting profanities to both Nick and Darren.

CHAPTER TWENTY

NICK BRACED HIS HANDS on his hips and looked after the gelding, who galloped toward the forest at full speed. Dean's crude swearing filled the night, and Nick grinned wolfishly.

Nick had decided to free Dean's hands and legs so that the boy could control the horse. However, the young man had thought to take advantage of Nick's generosity and attacked Nick once more as a way of payment.

That had forced Nick's hand, and he had to put Dean down with another well-aimed fist. This time though, Nick didn't want to leave the boy unconscious but only to subdue him. Unfortunately, in the process, Dean spat out two teeth, and consequently, he rode away with a bloody mouth.

'*He asked for that,*' Nick shrugged with indifference.

When the mount and rider disappeared in the forest, Nick turned and headed into the house. The man strode through the house in the direction of the basement with the intention of unchaining Darren.

Nick had mixed feelings about that. The young man seemed honest in his desire to not go back to Driscoll. But then, Nick was a cautious man and didn't trust anyone easily. Besides, he didn't want Darcy in any danger while she lived in his house, and Darrel might have posed a threat in the end.

Of course, Nick found Darren exactly where Nick had left the man. Still cuffed to the pipe, Darren couldn't have moved even if he had wanted.

Nick stopped next to the young man and stared at him. Darren's eyes filled with apprehension. The man moved his lips as if he wanted to say something but couldn't find his words.

"I'll take you into the house and put you into a bedroom. I'll take care of your wound in a short while, but I have something to do first," Nick said in a dry tone of voice and leaned over the man to unlock his handcuffs. Darren winced as if he thought that Nick would hit him.

"I don't beat defenseless men," Nick groused. He stuffed the handcuffs into his back pocket and then bent to help Darren up. "We'll have to climb two flights of stairs," Nick observed dryly. "Are you able to walk, or should I carry you?"

Darren's livid face became red with embarrassment. "I can walk," he replied weakly.

"We'll see about that," Nick retorted and steered the man toward the stairs.

By the time they reached the upper floor, Darren had sweated profusely and sagged entirely on Nick. The man wasn't featherlike, and Nick had to make efforts to support him all the way to the spare bedroom at the end of the hallway.

PULLED IN

On his way there, Nick noticed the spot on the corridor where Driscoll's man had made a fire to make him get out of the room. That made him reconsider things. It seemed that Driscoll had one man that walked like a ghost, and Nick didn't catch a whiff of him. He had to keep that in mind for his future plans.

Nick dropped the young man on top of the counterpane on the bed. Darren groaned but didn't comment. He didn't want to rouse the giant's fury.

"You'll have to wait here for a quarter of an hour probably. I'll be back to help you take your clothes off. I'll patch you up then," Nick informed him.

Darren just blinked to show that he heard Nick's words, but then he shut his eyes and sighed deeply with relief. The young man felt better lying on that bed than on the hard floor of the cellar.

Moreover, Darren was relieved to know that he wouldn't have to see Driscoll's darkened face or Gabe's ugly mug. He hoped never to see them again, but then, he was a realist. He knew that he couldn't avoid them if he remained in the area, even for a short while.

Nick headed to the door, and before shutting it behind him, he glanced back at Darren. The man seemed worn-out, and Nick shook his head. He hoped he hadn't made a mistake allowing Darren to remain behind. Nick stepped out of the room and shut the door behind him. Then, he also turned the key into the lock for security measures.

Satisfied with his actions, Nick hurried into his bedroom and opened the secret passage. He didn't even bother to look around and see what Driscoll's thugs had done to the room. Anyway, Nick didn't expect to find anything different from the rest of the house.

The man needed only a couple of minutes to reach Darcy's shelter. He knew the way by heart and didn't need to climb down the stairs slowly as he had done when he led Darcy there.

"Darcy, it's me," Nick shouted a few seconds before reaching the door of the shelter because he wanted to warn the young woman that he had returned.

Nick smiled when he heard the sound of the latch released from inside. Immediately, the door opened, and to Nick's surprise, Darcy hurried out of the room and jumped into his arms. She encircled Nick's neck with her arms tightly, and her legs latched to Nick's midriff. Darcy showed more strength than the man had believed she possessed.

Nick stumbled slightly under Darcy's weight, but he managed to slide his arms around her, and he gathered her to his chest. "Are you all right?" Nick inquired in a gruff tone of voice.

Darcy just nodded and glued her body to Nick's better. She hid her head in the crook of Nick's neck, and her fingers knotted in the back of the man's shirt.

Nick felt that the woman's body was shaking and decided to give her the time to recover. He knew it must have been hard for Darcy, locked inside the shelter, without the means of knowing what was going on in the cottage.

When Darcy's tears touched his skin, he sighed resignedly. Now he couldn't run anywhere to escape her tears, and besides, the woman clung to him like a vine.

"Everything is fine, Darcy. I told you so," Nick tried to make her quit crying.

Darcy just nodded, but her tears continued to soak the man's neck. Nick realized that he had to wait until she had spent her tears, and he closed his eyes with quiet resignation.

Slowly, Darcy's tension seeped out of her body. When she finally stopped crying, she wiped her face with her right hand, but she didn't look up at Nick. Darcy didn't want to see what the man was thinking about her blatant show of self-pity. However, she didn't unlatch her other hand or her legs from the man's body. Darcy held onto him as if Nick had been her lifeline.

"Are you better now?" Nick inquired. Then, he leaned back, as much as Darcy's arm allowed, and took a good look at her.

Darcy just nodded, but then she thought better and replied, "Yes, thank you. I'm sorry for this pitiful display."

"Don't worry about it," Nick patted her back tenderly. "However, we need to go back to the house," he informed her. "There's a guy in there who needs some medical care, and besides, I need to start planning."

"Emmett will come back, won't he?" Darcy asked, also leaning back to look into Nick's eyes.

"Yes," Nick replied briefly. The man didn't see the point in lying to Darcy. After all, the woman needed to be ready for anything.

Darcy pursed her lips and nodded. Then, she leaned forward and rested her head in the crook of Nick's neck again.

"Do you want me to carry you into the house?" Nick inquired quietly.

"Oh, no, sorry," Darcy hurried to say and climbed down the man's body. "You really look like a bear," Darcy noticed once she stood before Nick again.

Nick grinned but didn't reply. He just turned off the light in the shelter. Then he grabbed Darcy's hand and pulled her after him.

"By the way, all your hard work is gone," Nick thought to warn her. "The house is in shambles."

"They ransacked the house," Darcy concluded.

"Yep," Nick answered in a dry tone of voice.

"I'm sorry you had to suffer because of me," Darcy spluttered and bit her lower lip.

Nick stopped brusquely, and Darcy bumped into him. The woman looked up at him with inquiring eyes.

"You don't have to be sorry," Nick explained to her patiently. "You aren't guilty of what other people do. You got it?"

Darcy nodded hesitantly. Nick's reasoning seemed flawed somewhat, but the dark light in his coffee eyes stopped her from speaking up her mind. Of course, she was to blame. If she hadn't found shelter in Nick's house, Driscoll wouldn't have come to destroy the man's cottage.

PULLED IN

Nick noticed that his words hadn't swayed the woman's think, and his mouth turned into a hard line. He shook his head and then pulled her after him again. The man didn't have time to reason with Darcy just then. That would have to wait for a while.

CHAPTER TWENTY-ONE

"I DON'T KNOW HOW YOU feel about stab wounds, but I'd prefer that you come with me and take a look at the guy. You can tell me if you saw him before and what you know about him," Nick told Darcy when they came out of the secret passage.

"I haven't seen a stab wound before," Darcy replied, gazing at Nick. "But I can look at the man," she agreed.

Nick closed the panel to conceal the passage and turned to Darcy. He brushed his fingers through his hair and then waved his hand, inviting the woman to follow him.

They made a stop to get a bottle of alcohol Nick kept in a drawer in the salon, and they stopped again in the bathroom for other supplies that Nick needed to take care of Darren's wound.

Then, the two of them moseyed toward Darren's bedroom, and Nick unlocked the door. He stepped inside first, although he didn't think that Darren would be able to attack them. Still, Nick chose to be cautious.

Darren was still in bed, in the same position Nick had left him. The man turned his eyes toward the couple, and Nick observed that the man's pupils glistened with pain.

Nick laid the supplies he had brought with him on the night table. When he finished, he turned his head and glanced at Darcy. "So, have you seen him before?" he asked her.

Darcy nodded, but she showed some hesitation. "I think I saw him once. The first day, when Emmett showed me around the ranch. I think I noticed him then. He was with a few others at the stables," Darcy remembered, looking at Darren through narrowed eyes.

"That's true," Darren intervened. He scrambled to get into a sitting position, but a grimace appeared on his face, and he gave up. "Until today, I mostly guarded the stables," the man explained after he stifled a groan.

"Only the stables?" Nick inquired in a hard tone of voice and lifted his right brow, a clear sign that he didn't believe that.

Darren's face turned red, but he didn't reply. The man had detached himself from Driscoll's activities when he decided to run away. Yet, he didn't want to turn into a snitch.

"I see," Nick observed in a dry tone of voice. "You don't have to say anything," he put up his hand when Darren bit his lower lip, uncertain about what to do.

Nick arranged the things he had brought in a specific order on the night table. Then, his eyes turned toward Darcy, "You should leave now if you think that you're squeamish."

"I don't think I am," Darcy shook her head stubbornly and came closer to the bed. "And besides, you might need my help," she noted, and her eyes swept over the things that Nick had arranged on the nightstand.

"I can manage by myself," Nick waved his hand. "Don't worry about that. I'd prefer not to have to pick you up off the floor, though," Nick stared her down with hard eyes.

Darcy just stuck her tongue out, fed up with Nick's insistence. Nick's right brow lifted again, but with irony, this time, and Darcy blushed violently.

Darren's livid lips twitched when he observed Darcy's gesture. But then, he wondered at the woman's courage. Darren wouldn't have dared to confront Nick about anything. The man was built like a bear, and his sharp eyes made Darren wince every time Nick trained his gaze on him.

Nick noticed that Darcy didn't want to back down, so he returned to his ministrations. He helped Darren sit up and then started taking the young man's shirt off.

Coagulated blood had stuck the cloth to the man's back, and Darren hissed when Nick pulled it off without caution.

"Sorry, buddy," Nick said flatly. His tone of voice didn't convey any kind of regret. Nick had stitched his comrades many times in the past and learned to show indifference when faced with pain. It wasn't as if he could do anything to ease their discomfort.

Nick signaled to Darren to lie down on his belly, and the man hurried as much as possible to follow Nick's order, in spite of his body's stiffness. He didn't want to get on the giant's wrong side.

Darren already dreaded the patching process. He didn't believe that Nick would work with a nurse's featherlike hand. The man had already proved that he lacked any compassion.

Nick soaked a clean cotton towel in the bowl filled with hot water and disinfectant, which he had prepared before coming to Darren's room. He cleaned the wound carefully first, and then around the injury, turning a deaf ear at Darren's groans.

When he was satisfied that the wound and the skin around were as clean as they would ever be, Nick stepped back. He glanced at Darren's face and noticed that the man had blanched even more, and his mouth had contorted because of the pain.

"I know it hurts like hell, but we still have to disinfect it further. By the way, you are a lucky bastard. It is just a superficial stab, as I've already told you. The knife penetrated only the muscle and didn't go any deeper. I think the best thing would be to pour some alcohol over the wound. It will kill any bacteria that might still lurk inside," Nick told Darren. The man winced at Nick's words. He imagined that he would drown in a sea of pain once the alcohol made contact with the raw slash. Still, he nodded.

"Feel free to scream," Nick invited Darren in a casual tone of voice and grabbed the alcohol bottle he had placed on the night table. He unscrewed the lid and poured the alcohol liberally over the wound.

Darren screamed indeed, and Darcy clenched her hands together. She pressed her lips hard as if she could feel the man's agony.

"Now, it is clean," Nick approved of his handiwork after he made sure that he hadn't missed a spot. "I will sprinkle some powder antibiotic, and then I will patch you. You should be fine by tomorrow," he encouraged Darren, who had sagged on the bed, panting.

Nick was as good as his word, and in less than five minutes, he finished placing duct tape over Darren's stab wound so that it would close soon.

Darcy wondered at how nimble Nick's fingers were and concluded that the man had done that before and often enough.

Once he finished with patching Darren, Nick straightened and started gathering the things he had set on the night table. Before leaving the room, he turned to Darren, who was watching him with anxious eyes.

"I will not lock you inside the room," Nick announced Darren. "You will probably need to use the bathroom during the night. However, I would prefer that you didn't go downstairs. I can't trust you yet, and I hope you understand why," Nick said, throwing Darren a meaningful look.

Darren nodded briefly. He did understand the man's reasons, and he admitted that he would have done the same if he had been in Nick's shoes.

"I will make something for all of us to eat shortly," Nick continued. "Don't expect anything fancy or tasteful. Both Darcy and I seem to have deficiencies in this area," he explained.

Darcy gasped with outrage, and immediately Nick turned to her.

"What now?" he asked with exasperation.

"Your words," Darcy spluttered, pointing her finger to Nick in accusation.

"What about?" Nick shrugged. "I told him the truth. We can't promise a feast to the man. Most of the time, I don't even know whether my food would have a taste or not."

"Still..."

"There's no way around it, Darcy. I am a poor cook. You told me that you can't cook. Darren will have to eat our food. Where's the point in embellishing the truth?" Nick shrugged again.

"You're an impossible man," Darcy spluttered again, and turning her back to him, she went out of the room.

Nick stared at Darcy's retreating back and then turned to Darren. "Stay put. I will be back with some food soon. Try to rest," he advised the young man and then strode out, shutting the door behind him.

Nonetheless, Darren didn't hear Nick turn the key into the lock this time, and a grin tugged at the corners of his mouth.

CHAPTER TWENTY-TWO

WHEN NICK CAME OUT of Darren's room, Darcy was getting into her bedroom. Nick followed her with long strides. He put his hand on the door and stopped Darcy from shutting it in his face.

"We need to talk," Nick whispered, without giving any sign that he had noticed Darcy's frown. "Not here, but downstairs," he insisted, staring at the woman insistently.

Darcy would have liked to tell him to get lost, but she realized that her behavior would appear childish. She nodded her approval instead and waved her fingers toward the door, inviting Nick to lead the way out of the room. Nick started out, but he also grabbed Darcy's hand and pulled her in his wake.

"You know that this has become a habit for you," Darcy whispered furiously.

It wasn't the first time that Nick had just grabbed and pulled her. Right then, he wasn't on her list of favorite people. Nevertheless, the man just shrugged her words away with indifference and continued on his way.

"And this thing, shrugging, you do it all the time," Darcy whispered again with irritation.

"Are you keeping a list now?" Nick asked her, turning his eyes to her with curiosity. Nick gave up whispering because they had already reached his bedroom. Anyway, if Driscoll had planted Darren to play the role of a mole in Nick's household, their conversation wouldn't have helped Darren at all.

"Not really, but it isn't difficult to remember if you do it all the time," Darcy pointed out, in a normal tone of voice as well, shaking her head.

"Maybe," Nick accepted her conclusion with another shrug.

"Anyway, that's not the subject of discussion I had in mind," the man specified, looking at her pointedly, willing to get to more urgent business.

"I didn't think it would be," Darcy replied crossly. "But I believed that I should tell you about it. I don't really like being pulled here and there, without a word," she declared in a haughty tone of voice.

"Ah, I see. But you liked latching to me like a vine earlier," Nick retorted in a nasty tone of voice, and Darcy blushed.

"That happened in the heat of the moment," she explained. "I won't do it again. Don't worry."

"Actually, I didn't mind it. You should feel free to do it anytime," Nick replied and bobbed his eyebrows to her.

"You can dream, big boy," Darcy retorted and turned her nose up.

"What else do I have to do but dream?" Nick asked with good humor in his voice.

"How should I know what you should do with your time?" Darcy fired back.

PULLED IN

Nick burst into laughter and shook his head. "You don't give any quarter, Darcy. I like that in a woman," he said and brushed the side of the woman's face with the tips of his fingers. His coffee eyes looked straight into Darcy's with an alarming intensity.

The woman's pulse hastened, and she couldn't find her words anymore. She wasn't even able to gather her thoughts.

"You're something else, Darcy Burnett," Nick whispered with amazement, and leaning forward, he touched her lips with his mouth.

Darcy's lips parted slightly, and she sighed softly. Her eyes closed, and unconsciously, her fingers knotted in the man's shirt.

Nick didn't follow Darcy's mute invitation. He just brushed his lips to hers in a feather-like touch and then drew back.

Darcy's fingers let go of his shirt, and she opened her eyes. The man licked his lips and breathed deeply under the woman's widened eyes.

"Unfortunately, we have to discuss first," Nick repeated his earlier statement in a gruff tone of voice, and regret was written all over his features.

Darcy just nodded, unable to utter a sound. Her pulse had fastened, and butterflies fluttered in her belly.

Nick stepped back again so that he could fight temptation, yet his impenetrable eyes never left her face. For a moment, the man looked like he wanted to add something more. However, he just shook his head as if he changed his mind and decided to get to more practical matters.

"Come on, let's go to the kitchen to make some food. All that earlier commotion made me hungry," Nick explained. "We also need to talk and see what we should do so that in the future, we would not get in a situation similar to what we had this evening," he said, and his hand reached out to Darcy.

Still shaken to the core, Darcy timidly intertwined her fingers with Nick's and nodded. She followed the man outside, although her mind was still on the half chaste kiss they had shared just a few moments ago. It had jolted her to the core.

Nick noticed that the woman was pensive and refrained from adding anything more. The man didn't know what to say anyway. He couldn't explain his actions. Instinct had pushed him to kiss her. Nick headed to the stairs with Darcy in his wake. Halfway there, he changed his mind and stopped. Darcy bumped into him, and her eyes widened, asking him what had happened. Nick put his finger on her lips and then signaled to Darcy to stay where she was. He walked silently back to his room and returned in less than one minute with a roll of thin and transparent wire in his hand.

Nick invited Darcy to start down the stairs before him. He followed her but stopped on the top step. The man tied one end of the wire to one post of the rail at about two inches above the ground. Then he stretched the coil, cut off the excess, and fastened the other extremity to the opposite shaft. When he finished, Nick stepped down the stairs and looked critically at the wire. After a few seconds, he nodded with satisfaction and climbed down to reach Darcy. The woman had stopped halfway down and watched his actions with curiosity.

"Why?" she asked him in confusion.

"I am not convinced that Emmett Driscoll hadn't planted Darren into the house," Nick whispered and shrugged. "I think we'd better be prepared for anything. I hate being taken by surprise, and that already happened once tonight," he continued, upset with himself.

Nick took advantage of his position to interlace his fingers with Darcy's once more. The young woman's fingers trembled slightly in his, and he looked at her intently to see if his touch scared or disgusted her. He had never imposed his desire upon a woman.

A blush had powdered Darcy's cheekbones, and her pupils had dilated.

Nick didn't discern any anxiety in her appearance and grinned with satisfaction. '*Not bad, old man,*' he reflected.

"But... but what would that thing solve?" Darcy asked Nick in an uncertain tone of voice.

"Darren can't see it and wouldn't think I would do that. If he leaves his room and tries to come downstairs to take us by surprise, which I doubt, considering his state, he will stumble on the wire and fall down the stairs. If his intention is only to go to the bathroom, then everything's fine. Nothing will happen to him. Anyway, he shouldn't have any business to go anywhere else in the house," Nick pointed out in a hushed tone of voice.

"I see," Darcy murmured, slowly walking down next to Nick.

"What would you like for dinner?" Nick asked her in a normal tone of voice. A smile tugged at the corners of his mouth, and his fingers flexed over Darcy's encouragingly.

"Coq au vin and escargot," Darcy winked at him, and her lips turned up in a sassy smile.

"You imp," Nick laughed. "That you can get in your fancy dreams," he shook his head.

"You can choose between a beef stew, chicken stew, pork stew... Any choice you make, keep in mind that the product comes from a can, and all the vegetables are frozen. I haven't thought of taking some meat out of the freezer," he said in an apologetic tone of voice.

"Don't worry," Darcy shook her head. "Considering what I could make, I'm positive that your food will be excellent," she laughed.

Once in the kitchen, Nick left the wire roll on the counter and invited Darcy to take a seat at the kitchen table.

"I want to help you," Darcy shook her head. "I might not be good at cooking, but I can follow instructions very well," she told Nick.

"All right, but there's not much to do. I have only to open the meat cans and put the meat into the pan. I'm thinking of braising it with some onion and mushrooms first, then to add some water and frozen vegetables. What do you think?" Nick asked.

"It sounds good to me," Darcy replied with a shrug. "So, what should I do?"

"I have only one can opener so... I wouldn't trust you with slicing the onion, considering that you don't cook. So, I'll do that. You can put the pan on the stove with a bit of oil in it, I think," Nick suggested.

PULLED IN

"Meanwhile, I will open a wine bottle. It will help us to decompress a little. It is the only one I have, so I'd like you to sit down and savor it," Nick explained, taking the bottle out of the pantry and pulling the cork.

CHAPTER TWENTY-THREE

NICK BROUGHT A BOWL with steamy stew to Darren. He had also sliced some bread to pair it with the food.

"Can you eat where you are, or do you prefer that I help you to the table?" Nick asked Darren, tilting his head toward the table set in the corner of the room.

"I can eat here," Darren nodded, unwilling to make Nick carry him to the table.

"If you could only give me a hand to sit up..." the man asked Nick with embarrassment. Darren didn't think that he could move. Even the thought of handling the fork seemed a lot of work. It required energy he didn't have.

Nick just set the bowl filled with stew and the plate with bread on the night table, and then he grabbed Darren from under his arms and set him up.

Darren tried to smother his groans, but he was exhausted, and in spite of his efforts, he still squealed when Nick jarred his body.

"Sorry, buddy," Nick said without inflection. "It will take a couple of days to feel better again," he explained in an indifferent tone of voice. Then Nick handed the bowl with stew to the man, placing the plate with bread on the counterpane next to him afterward.

"I hope you like it," Nick said with a grimace. "Leave the bowl and plate on the night table or on the floor. What you think is more comfortable for you. I'll take them in the morning."

Darren nodded, and Nick left the room, leaving the man to *savor* the food.

Nick rushed to the kitchen, where Darcy waited for him.

"LET'S HAVE SOME MORE wine," Nick said and strode to Darcy, who sat at the table.

Darcy's eyes followed Nick's supple gait. A smile danced on her lips, and her pupils sparkled. Darcy had already had a glass of wine, and she showed the effects. A blush matted her cheekbones, and she seemed more relaxed than before. She nodded enthusiastically and lifted her glass so that Nick could pour her some more wine.

The man tilted his head and observed the woman carefully. "Are you sure you're all right?" he asked her with concern. Now the man questioned the wisdom of filling Darcy's glass again. She seemed to have had enough.

"I'm just great," Darcy directed a wide smile toward him and tapped the rim of the glass with one finger. "You said that you'd pour some more. What are you waiting for?"

"Probably for you to come back to your senses," Nick mumbled under his breath.

However, Darcy heard him and gasped as if the man injured her most sensible feelings.

"How can you say something like that?" she jumped off the chair and put the glass on the table with a thump.

Nick winced and stared at the glass with suspicion. He was almost sure that he would have to pick up shards off the table or the floor soon. That only if the woman hadn't thrown the glass directly to his head.

Darcy watched him with thunderous eyes and braced her hands on her hips. She had thrown her head back slightly, and her lips parted.

Nick had to admit that the woman looked magnificent, but still, she was drunk. He sighed and invited her to sit down again with a calm gesture. Darcy shook her head with determination, and Nick shrugged.

"If you want to stand, be my guest," Nick said. "If you also insist, I will pour you some more wine, but I'm afraid that this is not your regular poison, and tomorrow you'll feel the effects," he warned her without malice.

Darcy waved her hand toward the glass on the table, indicating that Nick should fill her glass. Nick sighed with resignation and served her once more.

"I don't know how much you still understand, but I need you to sleep in my bed tonight," the man said after he filled his glass as well and took a seat at the table.

Darcy's eyes widened, and her lips parted with astonishment. That was the last thing she had expected Nick to say. Interesting enough, she didn't know how she felt about his invitation, but she evidently wasn't repulsed, quite the opposite.

"It isn't what you think," Nick leaned forward and reassured her. "I only want to have you close to me if anything happens. I don't believe that Driscoll would come back tonight," he patted Darcy's hand when anxiety showed on her face suddenly. "Yet, there's still Darren to think about," he explained to her.

"If I am wrong about him, he may pose a problem. Do you understand what I am saying?" Nick sought confirmation from Darcy that she didn't take everything the wrong way.

"I won't touch you. You shouldn't worry about that. Anyway, you are too drunk. I prefer to make love to a woman who knows what I am doing and remembers everything in the morning," he added, and Darcy's brows bunched together.

The woman scowled at Nick, and the man grinned. However, he needed her approval, so he asked again, "Do we understand each other, Darcy?"

Darcy stared at him a few seconds and then nodded. She picked up her glass and took a mouthful as if she didn't drink anything for a long time.

Nick shook his head at a loss for words and sipped from his glass too. Then he picked up the phone he had left on the kitchen table earlier and speed-dialed a number under Darcy's inquiring eyes.

"Hi there, mate," Nick said when Ryan's voice boomed at the other end of the line. "Is everything fine?" he asked.

"Who's that?" Darcy asked him with suspicion, and her eyes narrowed dangerously.

"Who are you talking to?" the woman inquired again, and her agitation amplified. She seemed ready to jump out and run out of the house.

PULLED IN

Nick glanced at her, although he continued to listen carefully to his friend's words. "Ryan, give me a second," he suddenly said when he realized that Darcy's fear was evident and escalating.

"Darcy, I am just talking to my friend, Ryan. You don't have anything to fear," he pointed out, trying to make her calm down.

However, Darcy didn't seem to believe him. She even shook her head, rejecting his reassuring words.

"If I put the phone on speaker, will you feel better?" Nick asked her with concern.

Darcy seemed to ponder his proposition for a couple of seconds and then nodded, even though she didn't look very convinced that his solution would help.

"I'm putting you on speaker, Ryan. It's not a problem because Darcy is directly involved in everything," Nick explained to his friend.

"I gather that you are in a sort of situation there," Ryan's poised voice came on the line.

"Yes, Ryan. I am. I wouldn't have called you at this hour otherwise. I imagine you have better things to do than talk to me. However, I need help in making some plans," Nick said. "You know I've never been a good strategist, anyway," he thought to add.

"Don't worry about that, mate," Ryan replied. "Just tell me what's going on, and we'll come up with something," he encouraged Nick.

Nick succinctly explained how Darcy came to his ranch and what happened afterward. He took also care to detail Driscoll's background and reach in the area so that Ryan had a full picture of the situation.

"I understand," Ryan replied in a hard tone of voice.

"You don't need just strategy, Nick. You need substantial help. You won't be able to keep that guy at bay by yourself," Ryan concluded.

"I can't ask that from you or Adam," Nick shook his head as if Ryan could see him. "You have the two little munchkins to take care of, and I spoke to Adam a couple of weeks before, and he told me that Diane had just got pregnant."

"Don't worry about any of that, friend," Ryan dismissed Nick's concerns. "Even so, we can be there for you. After all, you were always there for us when we needed it."

"I didn't do it so that I could ask you to return the favor," Nick retorted slightly outraged.

"I haven't said that," Ryan replied to Nick in a calm tone of voice. "Let me talk with Adam first, and I'll call you back in the morning with more information," Ryan asked.

Nick didn't say a thing for a few moments. He closed his eyes and reflected on Ryan's words, and the tension permeated the telephone line.

"Are you still there, mate?" Ryan's voice came through with concern.

Nick shook his head to clear it and opened his eyes. His gaze met Darcy's confused look, and that helped him make his decision. It wasn't about his pride, after all. He needed to keep her safe.

"Yes, Ryan, do that. Speak to Adam and get back to me when you can," Nick said with determination.

"In the morning, brother," Ryan replied and disconnected the call.

Nick picked up his glass and sipped pensively, gazing in the distance. Darcy observed him, biting her lower lip. She brimmed with trepidation. When she couldn't stand the suspense anymore, Darcy leaned over the table and touched the back of Nick's hand.

Nick's eyes shifted to her and noticed her worry. It was evident that she was unsure of what was going on and needed his reassurance. Nick took Darcy's fingers in his hand, and his thumb stroked the edge of her palm.

"You needn't worry about anything, Darcy. Everything will turn out fine," he said softly. "Ryan will bring Adam, and with the three of us here, you have nothing to fear. I promise. We all have the necessary skills to deal with such situations," he reassured Darcy.

Darcy nodded, although her face showed some hesitation. She wasn't very sure about the skills that Nick and his friends had acquired. She didn't know any of them to make an opinion. Still, the good thing was that Nick's conversation with Ryan had sobered Darcy almost entirely. "I think we should go to bed," the woman practically whispered. "It is almost dawn," Darcy observed, glancing toward the window.

The faint light outside showed that night was already giving way to the day, and dawn was upon them. Tension and tiredness combined with the effects of the wine, and Darcy felt her eyes drop.

"All right, come on," Nick pulled Darcy's fingers gently. "You'll sleep in my bed, and no, this is not a come on," he made sure to point out when he noticed her widened eyes. "Still, you'll stay in my room as long as Darren is here, and until this situation is resolved," Nick insisted. Then he pulled Darcy up and helped her to walk toward the door.

CHAPTER TWENTY-FOUR

DARCY WINCED AND WOKE up cursing. She yawned, mostly with annoyance. That persistent ringing in her ears had eventually managed to ruin her sleep, although she had done her best to ignore it. Darcy's head was pounding, and her eyes stung.

'*That damn wine,*' Darcy reflected.

She experienced the effects of a full hangover, and nausea rose in her throat alarmingly, making her swallow hard.

The woman rubbed her eyes with sluggish moves. Darcy looked around and discovered that she was alone, both in bed and in the room.

"Take care of me, huh," Darcy muttered, disappointed to see that Nick had left her alone in there. "You insisted that I'd sleep in your bed so that you could protect me, and now you've gone God knows where and left me to fend for myself if something happened," she continued to mutter. Then Darcy turned her back to the door and to the bothering sound coming from the night table on Nick's side of the bed.

"Who left you alone?" Nick's gruff voice came from the door.

Darcy turned around quickly and winced. '*Damn, I shouldn't have done that,*' she thought. A sharp pain pierced her brain, and Darcy closed her eyes. Suddenly, she got dizzy.

The woman groaned and propped her head in her hand, afraid that it would fall off. At least, it felt that way. After a few seconds, she opened her eyes again, and she gasped. Her eyes practically popped out of their sockets when they laid on Nick.

The man had just closed the door behind him, and now he strode with giant steps to the nightstand to reach the offending ringing cell phone, which had roused Darcy from her slumber.

The man wore nothing else but a small towel around his hips. The cloth stopped at half his thigh and parted at every step the man took, revealing his muscular legs.

'*This is definitely a man who's used to exercising,*' Darcy concluded. She swallowed hard while savoring the dance of the sunlight on the hard planes of the body displayed before her wide eyes.

A slight grin tugged at the corners of Nick's mouth when he noticed Darcy's apparent interest in his physique. The woman had forgotten everything about her earlier complaints or that Nick had asked something.

"Talk to me," Nick said, answering the phone call. Recalling Darcy's concerns from the previous night, Nick put the phone on speaker and left it on the nightstand. Then he waved his hand toward Darcy, inviting her to turn around.

"I need to get dressed, sweetheart. If you don't want a clear view of my private bits, you should turn your eyes away," he whispered gruffly, and Darcy hurried to do just that.

However, she wasn't fast enough, and Nick had the time to notice the blush covering the woman's entire face and even the tips of her ears and her neck.

"I still can hear you, Nick," Ryan's voice, filled with laughter, boomed into the room.

"So what?" Nick said with indifference, taking a pair of briefs from one of the drawers and pulling them on.

Ryan's manly laugh made Darcy wince. Someone with a drum had taken residence in her brain and was giving a full-blown concert now. Darcy's face turned a deeper shade of scarlet because of Ryan's words.

However, Nick merely continued to get dressed with economical gestures and didn't comment. "You can turn back, Darcy. I'm decent now," Nick called out to her. "You can talk to me anytime if you finished laughing, Ryan," Nick said in a deceptively mild tone of voice. Still, Darcy perceived the underlining steel in the man's words.

Then Kate's whispers reached Nick's ears, and he grinned. He had always liked Ryan's wife and found her brave and soft at the same time.

"Hi there, Kate," Nick greeted her, and to Darcy's bewilderment, the man's face softened. Suddenly, she felt jealous of that Kate she didn't know.

"Hi there, Nick," a throaty young female voice replied. "We'll see each other soon," she warned the man playfully, and laughter sounded in her voice. "I can't wait. It's been too long," she said.

Darcy tightened her teeth. Not only a sharp pain crossed her brain when the other woman's voice reached her ears, but she also didn't like to hear that Kate couldn't wait to lay her eyes on Nick.

"What about the munchkins?" Nick asked with astonishment. He wouldn't have thought that Kate would come with Ryan to Montana and leave the children at home.

About a year and a half ago, Kate and Ryan had been blessed with twins, a boy, and a girl, and Ryan's most ardent wish came true. Ryan became a father while he was still young and able to keep up with the children. The boy, Aiden, had taken after his mother and possessed a sweet disposition most of the time. God forbid to get on his wrong side, though. His wrath was something out of the horror books.

The girl, Andrea, had taken after her father. She had inherited her father's adventurous spirit and fiery temper, and she was giving fits of fright to her parents all the time. Ryan was sure he would turn white before his time.

Although Kate and Ryan periodically told him about the twins' adventures, Nick had chanced to see the toddlers for the last time when they celebrated their first anniversary. At that time, Nick had left one of his neighbor's sons to take care of his ranch, and he had traveled to Montreal for an entire week. He had actually done the same when Kate gave birth to them because Ryan had needed his friends' moral support.

Worries and insecurity had overwhelmed him, and Ryan had turned into a brainless man.

The two imps had charmed Nick, and he had felt like an honorific uncle. Kate and Ryan had assured both Nick and Adam that they really were the children's uncles.

"We've made arrangements for the kids," Ryan replied in a hard tone of voice, betraying the fact that in reality, he hadn't categorically agreed with those arrangements.

Nick understood immediately that probably Ryan had had a heated argument with Kate about that and lost. Nick knew his friend well and wouldn't have expected Ryan to bring his wife willingly with him in the middle of a potentially explosive situation.

But then, Nick knew Kate as well, and when an idea got into Kate's head, Ryan couldn't make her change her mind no matter what. No one could.

"Yes, Nick," Kate's voice intervened. "We arranged with Mark and Jeanne to take turns babysitting the twins."

"Ouch," Nick exclaimed, and a grimace appeared on his face. "I imagine you're not very satisfied with the arrangement, Ryan," Nick guessed.

Mark used to be their boss when Ryan, Nick, and Adam worked for special ops. Nick doubted that Mark had the slightest idea about taking care of toddlers. Nick, for one, had never heard the man talking about children.

"You said it, brother," Ryan replied in a dry tone of voice.

"Come on, stop your whining, Ryan," Kate interfered. "The situation is well in hand. Jeanne will be here, after all, and she'll know what to do and take care of the children if Mark isn't capable."

Nick's ear caught Ryan's deep breathing and grinned. Kate had always had a special gift to make Ryan run in circles if she wanted.

"Anyway, Adam and Diane will be with you in about three or four hours. They left early this morning, a couple of hours after I spoke to them," Ryan informed Nick.

"Is Adam bringing Diane too?" Nick asked with bewilderment. "But she's..."

"I know," Ryan interrupted him. "She's pregnant. However, Adam didn't stand a chance. Diane can't wait to meet both your guest and Kate, so she didn't want to hear anything about her remaining behind," he explained. His tone of voice revealed what he thought about the arrangement.

"I see," Nick mumbled. "I suppose Adam is not very happy right now, and he resents that he had to come here because of me."

"Be serious," Kate replied in a harsh tone of voice. "Diane is just pregnant, for God's sake. She's not even in three months yet. It's not like she's got a terminal illness, guys. Diane can function just fine," Kate continued bitingly. "I've been there, and I know how it is."

Nick didn't know what to say to that. He exchanged a look with Darcy, but the woman merely shrugged.

Darcy couldn't help him. She didn't know the people involved, so she couldn't have an opinion about anything Nick discussed with his friends.

Nevertheless, Darcy thought that Diane could come to visit Nick in spite of Driscoll's presence. Only if she had some pregnancy complications, Diane would have been in trouble.

"Anyway," Ryan interrupted the tense silence, "Kate and I will arrive later tonight. I've just got a charter flight from Montreal to Great Falls early this afternoon and arranged to rent a car when we get there. I can't guarantee how soon that will be, though. We might arrive around 19:00 this evening or a little earlier," he explained.

Nick breathed deeply and said, "Thank you, Ryan. I'll feel better once everyone is here."

"Don't mention it, buddy. We are and will always be a team," Ryan replied in a positive tone of voice. "See you soon," he added and disconnected the call.

Nick only nodded and grabbed the cell phone to shove it into his pocket with a pensive look on his face. After a few moments, he turned to Darcy and said, "Let's take care of breakfast. Maybe you won't feel so bad afterward."

Then the man thought better and added in a sober tone of voice, "I suppose you'd like to shower first. I'll wait in front of the bathroom door until you take your shower," Nick decided.

"Huh," Darcy snorted and threw her legs over the edge of the bed.

"What now?" Nick asked the woman, looking at her through narrowed eyes and bracing his hands on his hips.

Darcy waved her hand dismissively, got out of the bed, and headed toward the door, a hand on her head. She didn't seem steady on her legs either.

"No, really, what?" Nick insisted, following her, ready to catch her if she fell. He had noticed the woman's dizziness but chose not to comment about that.

"You left me alone in the bedroom earlier," Darcy suddenly turned to him, her eyes thundering. "It's a bit too late to think about guarding the bathroom door while I shower, don't you think?" Darcy huffed.

"I might have left you alone in the bedroom, but I locked Darren in his room before going to shower. I also set up a little trap on the stairs. By the way, I should take care of it now, because otherwise..." Nick said, waving his hand. "Once you've finished with your shower, I'll unlock Darren's room so that he could visit the bathroom as well. I am also going to give you something for your hangover when we get downstairs," the man offered with a small smile on his lips.

Nick didn't miss the pain shining in Darcy's pupils and imagined that she had a hell of a time.

"I've got a concoction that tastes awful, but I can swear by it. The guys have tried it several times, and it worked like magic. You'll feel like new in no time. You'll see."

Darcy turned her nose up but blushed. She couldn't contest the fact that she had a hangover. A few guys with hammers and anvils had joined the drummer in her head, and she felt like screaming.

Darcy had never been in such a situation before. Coffee and soft drinks were her poisons, and she had drunk only beer without alcohol.

'And I'd better stick to those,' she reflected. She didn't want a repeat of that experience.

Darcy thought that Nick's concoction might help regardless of how bad the taste. Anyway, she didn't believe that anything would have tasted good right then. She couldn't wait to brush her teeth and get rid of the aftermath of her last night's indulgence.

CHAPTER TWENTY-FIVE

ADAM DROVE INTO NICK'S ranch yard around noon. This time, the motion sensor devices had already warned Nick that someone was coming. That morning, the man had made a tour and checked every sensor, and now he could rely on them. All of them functioned as he expected.

However, Nick knew that anything could happen and had taken out a few weapons from his arsenal. He wanted them at hand if he needed them.

Once the warning that someone had breached the line of the property came, Nick got ready to take action. He went out of the house armed with a Taser rifle and two semi-automatic guns to welcome the visitors. He had hidden them in the hallway closet near the front door just before lunchtime.

Adam noticed the weapons and burst into laughter. He shook his head and honked, waving at Nick through the car window.

He drew the car closer to the ranch house and then jumped out of the car, stretching his legs and flexing his shoulders.

"I hope that you don't consider to shoot me with that Taser rifle, mate," Adam laughed heartily. Then he strode around the hood to open the car door for Diane.

"Diane prefers that I don't twitch. Are you all right, pumpkin?" Adam solicitously asked his wife, giving her his hand and helping her step out of the car.

"Why wouldn't I be?" Diane replied in a negligent tone of voice.

Diane took Adam's hand, unconcerned. She knew that she couldn't show any weakness or tiredness before her husband right then.

Adam was concerned about Diane's well-being as a rule but had started worrying about her health more than before since she got pregnant. Diane didn't want to bank the fire of the man's fears. In spite of his bold attitude, Adam turned into an old woman, distressed about everything when it came to Diane.

Adam had forcefully declared that he was against Diane's coming with him. The man had yielded and accepted that he couldn't dictate her moves only after a very vocal fight, which lasted for about two hours that morning, right after dawn.

Sometimes, arguing with Adam was exhausting, so Diane didn't want a repeat that day. Moreover, now she was tired, indeed, after the long ride across Montana.

When Diane emerged from the car, Nick shoved the two pistols into the belt of his pants and hung the rifle over his shoulder. He hurried down the stairs and headed directly to Diane. He reached the couple, pushed Adam aside without ceremony, and crushed the woman in his arms.

"Hey, hey, man," Adam shouted at him with vexation. "Let her be. You're smothering her, you, crazy bear," he snapped at Nick and slapped him hard over the shoulder.

"You wouldn't like it if I did the same thing to your woman," Adam observed and glowered at his friend, his black eyes thundering with anger.

"I'm fine, Adam, don't make so much fuss," Diane tried to calm the waters once Nick let go of her. "I haven't known you are so demonstrative, though," she beamed at Nick, patting his arm tenderly.

"Well, you know that I haven't seen you in a long while, sweetheart," Nick shrugged with nonchalance. "Plus, I found out that congratulations are in order," he added with a meaningful look at Diane's midriff.

He grabbed one of Diane's hands between the two of his with care as if he were afraid that the woman's delicate bones would break under his fingers.

"In that case, you should try to smother me too," Adam pointed out maliciously. "After all, I had a huge contribution to Diane's present state," he made sure to mention and winked at Diane.

"Adam," Diane shouted, and her face turned scarlet. "You always like to put me in embarrassing situations in front of Nick," she said.

Diane remembered well the time when she had laid eyes on Adam's friend for the first time. She hadn't forgotten Adam's comments on that occasion.

Nick had come to Diane's ranch to help Adam to keep her safe. Someone wished not only to put their hand on Diane's land but also wanted her dead.

Nick waved his hand to chase Diane's concerns away and turned to Adam.

"With your ugly mug, no one would want to smother you with hugs," Nick said in a dry tone of voice, but a bright light gleamed in his eyes. Then, only to contradict his own words, Nick burst into laughter and caught Adam in a bear hug. He thumped his friend on his back vigorously, happy to see him after more than a year. Nick had missed Adam's acerbic wits and irreverence.

"I appreciate the enthusiasm," Adam said, trying to step back. "However, I'm not a rug, man. You needn't try so hard to dust me. I promise to take a shower soon," he grinned at Nick, showing his big white teeth.

"You've always been a clown," Nick observed with a shake of his head and thumped Adam once more, just for fun. "Let me introduce you to Darcy," he said and turned toward Darcy.

The woman had halted on top of the stairs leading to the veranda. Nick had spotted her coming out of the house a few minutes earlier when she realized that there was no danger. Nick waved his fingers to Darcy, inviting her to join the group.

Hesitantly, Darcy moseyed to them, eying Diane suspiciously. She found the woman too attractive with her lively coppery hair and green eyes, and suddenly she felt frumpy next to Diane. Moreover, Darcy had noticed that Nick looked at Adam's wife with tenderness, and she didn't like it.

Darcy was envious because the man had never glanced at her that way. Sometimes, his eyes shone with strong emotion when Nick stared at her. However, Darcy wasn't quite sure what it meant, and she worried that she might misunderstand his feelings for her.

PULLED IN

Nick sensed that something was wrong with Darcy, but he didn't have the time to dwell on her behavior right then and find an explication. So, he chose to think that she was just shy in a new company, and to boost her confidence, he took the woman's hand and pulled her close to him.

"Diane, Adam, this is Darcy," Nick introduced her to his friends. He waved his hand between them, and then, he turned to Darcy and said to her, a broad smile on his lips, something she hadn't seen before, "These are two of my best friends, sweetheart. You'll meet the other two this afternoon."

"You mean to say that we are your only friends," Adam elbowed Nick and grinned. "No one else would stand this solitary bear," Adam turned to Darcy and whispered comically to her.

Nick returned the favor by placing a very well-aimed elbow in his side and making Adam groan. However, he didn't bother to contradict his friend.

The man was right, after all. Nick didn't have any other friends besides Adam, Ryan, and their wives. He loved his solitude and didn't need other people in his life, although Darcy's presence had made him reconsider his choices.

Still, Nick didn't know if his decision to alter his ways referred only to that specific woman, and he couldn't analyze his reasoning right then. Unfortunately, other things took precedence.

Nick didn't make friends quickly. He didn't trust people, so he preferred having acquaintances, who didn't ask much of his time. They were satisfied with drinking a beer with Nick now and then or playing a poker game once in a blue moon.

Darcy looked up at Nick's face, and the lights in his dark brown eyes confused her. A small smile trembled on her lips and betrayed her hesitation. She didn't know what to make of Nick's or Adam's behavior.

Diane reached out at her immediately, intending to reassure her, and shook Darcy's hand. The young woman seemed out of her element between the two men, and Diane knew from experience that the men's presence and behavior could be overwhelming at the beginning. It took some time to get used to them.

"I'm so happy to meet you, Darcy," Diane said and smiled widely at the small blue-eyed, dark-haired woman, who was clinging to Nick's hand with all her might now.

'My God, such cobalt eyes,' Diane reflected, staring at Darcy's unusual eye color.

Colored by jealousy, Darcy's initial impression of Diane hadn't been favorable. However, now the kindness shining in the woman's green eyes encouraged Darcy to take Diane's hand and shake it.

"You can't imagine how long I've been waiting for this day," Diane continued to say. She shook her head in bewilderment and laughed. "I almost despaired of seeing this lonely man with a woman at his arm," she remarked playfully, shifting her sparkling green eyes toward Nick. "You even refused to come with someone at my wedding or when Kate baptized her babies. I thought you would turn into a monk," she teased Nick and winked at him.

"It's not what you think," Nick replied in a dry tone of voice. "Darcy is just my guest," he contradicted Diane.

Still, a small voice at the back of his mind told him that he was lying to himself. Darcy had stopped being a mere guest for him, and that soon after her arrival. He wasn't sure about his feelings yet, but a shift had taken place in how he felt and reasoned.

"Yeah, yeah, yeah," Adam waved Nick's words dismissively. "I bet she is," he whacked Nick over the shoulder. "And I also bet my last white t-shirt that she spent last night with you in your bed," Adam grinned mischievously at his friend first.

Then he trained his piercing eyes onto Darcy as if he wanted to ferret out all her secrets.

The young woman blushed violently under Adam's prying dark eyes. Subtly, she tried to disengage her hand from Nick's, afraid that people might get some wrong ideas. Nick didn't let go of her hand, although he had noticed Darcy's discomfort. He bad-mugged Adam, ready to give him a harsh retort for his lack of tact.

"I'm hungry," Diane declared in an imperative tone of voice. She wanted to put an end to the staring contest between Adam and Nick. The men measured each other with hard eyes as if they were two rabid duelists out on the field at dawn.

At Diane's words, Darcy's eyes shifted toward Nick with alarm. She forgot utterly about Adam's observations when she realized that she hadn't thought that Nick's friends would need something to eat. Now, she felt like slapping herself silly.

'How stupid can I be?' she wondered. 'Of course, people need to eat. They come all the way here, so, at least, we should feed them.'

Nick felt Darcy's fingers tightening over his and noticed that she didn't know what to do or how to answer to Diane. The man shook his head at Darcy. Then he stroked her hand, letting her know that she shouldn't fret about it. After all, he had everything well in hand.

'*Sort of*,' he thought.

However, he didn't have the time to intervene. At Diane's words, Adam had immediately slid an arm around his wife as if she were in immediate danger of fainting because of a lack of food. Then he turned to Nick, asking in a commanding tone of voice, "Is there any food at the ready? Diane needs something to eat, and now."

"Diane won't wither and die if she waits for a few minutes, though," Diane said mockingly and shook her head at Nick, a smile turning up the corners of her mouth.

Nick sighed inwardly. He knew that Adam wouldn't be satisfied with what they had to offer to Diane for lunch. However, he answered with confidence, "I made some stew last night, and there's still some of it left on the stove."

"Is it you who made it?" Adam grimaced with disgust. "Blah! His food has never been popular, and you'll see soon why," he confessed to Diane with regret. "My wife needs something better," he said in an authoritative tone of voice, his eyes turning back to Nick.

"I'm sure we'll survive just fine with what Nick has cooked," Diane replied dryly, annoyed with Adam's comment.

"You've eaten my food before, and you're still here," Nick reminded Adam with animosity.

"That doesn't mean I didn't complain. I hope you remember that. And Diane is special. She can't eat your concoction. She's pregnant, man. Don't you cook?" Adam suddenly turned to Darcy.

The woman froze, and her eyes widened. A faint blush spread on her face and neck.

"She doesn't need to cook," Nick interceded immediately in a harsh tone of voice.

He slid an arm around the woman and gathered her to his side. He refused to let anyone make Darcy feel inadequate for something as trivial as cooking.

Food was food, after all. Even Diane's pregnancy wouldn't suffer any side effects if she ate what he had cooked. The stew was relatively fresh, and this time, luckily, it had some taste.

CHAPTER TWENTY-SIX

THE TWO COUPLES STEPPED into the kitchen, and Adam thumped Nick over the shoulder with enthusiasm. "I like it, man. You've got a nice ranch house here."

Adam's voice started Darren, and he dropped the empty bowl he was carrying to the sink. The dish fell on the wooden floorboards and broke into pieces.

Everyone's eyes shifted from the slivers on the floor to the young man, and Adam's brows rose mockingly.

Darren stared at the two couples as well and bit his lower lip with apprehension. He had frozen on the spot and didn't know what to do. The man was also concerned about what Nick would think about his moving around the kitchen.

Darren was aware that Nick didn't trust him at all and preferred that Darren hadn't moved freely through the house. It wasn't difficult to observe that. Nick didn't miss any chance to lock the young man in his bedroom.

When he got the signal that someone was coming, Nick had left Darren at the kitchen table, ordering him not to move.

At the time, Darren dug into a bowl filled with the stew that Nick had laid before him around lunchtime. However, after Darren waited for a while, curiosity took the best of him. He itched to see what was going on outside, so he hurried and finished eating his lunch. The man intended to go to a window to look out, afraid that Driscoll or Gabe had returned. He didn't know what he could have done in that situation, but he would have thought of something.

Darren had been so focused on standing up in spite of the stabbing pains he felt in his back that he missed the steps of the four people approaching the kitchen. The apparition of the group surprised him.

When Darren's eyes met Adam's, his mouth turned into a thin line. He hadn't known that someone else was coming to help Nick and Darcy. Nick frightened Darren enough, but the unknown man he had before his eyes seemed harsher and more ruthless than Nick.

Darren lowered his eyes, and only then he realized that he had broken the bowl. Embarrassment showed in his eyes, and the man thought to gather the shards on the floor, but Nick waved at him away, urging him to sit back down in his chair.

Adam's hard eyes searched the young man's face carefully and then shifted toward Nick inquiringly. One of Adam's brows rose on his forehead, asking Nick mutely who that guy was.

Nick had noticed the unpleasant exchange between the two men and Adam's reaction to the addition to his household, but he didn't comment. Instead, he chose to introduce Darren to others.

"Diane, Adam, this is Darren. He is one of the other night's invaders. Apparently, he decided to distance himself from Driscoll's actions, or at least, that's what he claims," Nick said in a hard tone of voice. He trained his gaze on Darren's face to warn the young man that he would pay if he had lied to him.

Darren caught his lower lip between his teeth but still found the gumption to nod toward the two newcomers.

Diane smiled at the man, but uncertainty fluttered on her lips. She didn't see the wisdom in keeping a man from the adverse band in the house. Still, she decided against asking Nick about his reasons to allow Darren to stay there.

Adam just nodded briefly toward Darren, and his dark eyes promised a lot of pain to the man if he betrayed Nick's trust.

Adam had known Nick for a long time and never thought that the man had been milquetoast. Nick had proved ruthless when he fought side by side with Adam and Ryan.

Adam suspected that Darcy's arrival in Nick's life might have altered the man's judgment.

Darcy bent to pick up the broken pieces off the floor, but Nick stopped her at once, putting his hand on her shoulder. "I will take care of that, sweetie," he whispered to her, pulling her up and sliding an arm around her. He led her to a chair at the table and helped her to sit down. Afterward, Nick also invited Diane and Adam to have a seat at the table. Once he was satisfied that everyone was sitting down, Nick picked up the broken pieces off the floor and threw them in the garbage bin. Then he strode to the stove to bring the pot with stew to the kitchen table.

Darcy thought of making herself useful, and she rushed to take the plates and cutlery from the cupboard, despite Nick's wish that she should only sit and wait. *'I won't break if I carry on such a simple task,'* she grimaced inwardly, annoyed with Nick's constant care. However, in a way, the man's behavior made her feel cherished.

Once Nick laid the food before them, Diane and Adam started eating, although with some reluctance.

"It's not so bad," Adam admitted with mild surprise after the first bite.

His eyes widened, and he shook his head in bewilderment. "You made worse food if you remember. That dog in Salvador comes to mind," he teased Nick, who scowled at his friend. "Not even he wanted to eat your so-called stew. Well, it seems that your talents improved, brother. Not much, but still, there's a definite improvement," he offered some backhanded praise to his friend.

Nick just showed him his finger but didn't think of getting into a full-blown argument with Adam. There were ladies present, after all.

Darcy offered to make some coffee or tea, but everyone refused. Diane and Adam continued eating, while Darcy, Darren, and Nick waited for them to finish.

No one knew what to say. Darren's presence among them restricted the conversation subjects, and the silence in the kitchen turned heavy.

"So, how was your trip here?" Nick asked just to fill in the silence.

Adam shrugged, and after he swallowed, he said, "Not bad. A bit too long for Diane, I'm afraid. But then, I couldn't make her understand that she should remain at home, could I?" he turned his hard eyes to his wife. He shook his head and glanced upward as if he were at a loss of words.

PULLED IN

The criticism in his tone of voice and eyes was unmistakable, and Diane kicked him from under the table. Adam's bewildered eyes turned to her, wordlessly asking what had happened.

"Don't pretend you don't know why I kicked you," she glowered at Adam. "I'm sick and tired of hearing the same thing all over again," she said and gestured with her fork to him, splashing him with clumps of stew in the process. "You've done that all the way here. Enough is enough," she snapped at him.

Nonplussed, Adam wiped off his face and mumbled with annoyance, "Will you have some care with that fork?"

"Maybe you'd like to see how you look wearing my bowl," Diane bit back, and she seemed more than ready to be faithful to her words.

Darcy watched the exchange wide-eyed, expecting that things would escalate any moment now. Her father had been a quiet man, and regardless of how much her mother harped, he had never replied back. Still, later, she had witnessed full-blown exchanges with insults and broken dishes whenever her mother's relationships went down the drain.

As Darcy didn't have women friends, she wasn't aware that such banter was part of a relationship. A quarrel didn't mean that things would start flying around, so the argument between Diane and Adam scared her.

Nick sensed Darcy's distress and placed his hand over hers. His fingers stroked hers to reassure the young woman that everything was all right. He knew his friends and had witnessed such bickering in the past. Diane was more than capable of withstanding Adam's acerbic personality, and Adam wouldn't have done anything to hurt her.

Diane noticed Darcy's anxiety and put her left hand on Adam's knee. She shook her head to him, and the man frowned for a few seconds, not understanding what was going on. Diane tilted her head slightly toward Darcy. Adam turned to the woman and winced inwardly. Her face was pale, and he read apprehension in her pupils.

"Nick will tell you that you have nothing to fear, Darcy," Adam in a grave tone of voice. "Diane and I enjoy arguing, but that doesn't mean we don't respect each other or that we would get into physical fights," he pointed out.

Darcy just flipped her hand. She didn't know what to reply. She glanced from Darcy to Adam, and then, her eyes turned to Nick, who watched Darcy with the same intense passion that she had seen before.

Reading the questions in Darcy's eyes, Nick just shrugged. His fingers flexed on hers, and in the spur of the moment, he lifted her hand to his mouth. Turning her palm up, he pressed it to his lips.

Darcy gasped, and her fingers quivered in Nick's hand. Her pupils dilated, swallowing most of the cobalt of her iris. Butterflies danced in her belly, taking her by surprise.

Nick noticed both her surprise and arousal. He grinned and brushed his lips over her skin once more. A mischievous light sparked in his eyes and challenged Darcy to refute his gesture. She only licked her lips, unable to say anything.

Darcy was unsure of almost everything. However, she didn't doubt that she enjoyed feeling the man's lips on her hand and didn't mind his bolder approach.

Diane and Adam witnessed the interlude between Darcy and Nick, and they exchanged a meaningful look and a smile. Darren just looked away, feeling like a voyeur.

Darcy and Nick seemed to have forgotten about the others. They merely stared at each other. Both realized that the boundaries between a host and his guest had fallen away. Surprised that things had turned that way, neither Darcy nor Nick knew how to act for the moment.

"I'd like to eat something sweet," Adam suddenly intervened. He felt somewhat embarrassed to observe that intense flux of unspoken feelings between Nick and Darcy, especially because Adam had never seen his buddy reacting that way.

"I'm sure that Diane would like some too," Adam insisted when no one paid any attention to him.

Diane pinched him to shut up, and Adam turned to her peevishly. "What now? Don't tell me you don't want something for dessert," he said gruffly.

Finally, Nick's eyes shifted to Adam and watched him with curiosity. Then he understood what happened to his friend and grinned.

"No problem, brother," he said. "I'm sure there are a few cans of stewed peach in the pantry. You're welcome at it," Nick assured Adam, and after he kissed Darcy's fingers once more, he stood up. He stroked the woman's shoulder tenderly and asked her, "Would you like some too?"

Darcy just nodded with uncertainty. She hadn't processed the shift in her relationship with Nick yet.

"Darren?" Nick asked the young man who watched the cupboard intently.

"I'm sorry," Darren replied. "What did you ask?"

"I asked if you wanted some peach compote," Nick repeated patiently.

"Yes, thank you," the young man said. Nevertheless, the thought that he would have preferred to be anywhere else but in that kitchen. The level of testosterone was high even for him, and he was used to living in barracks with the men.

CHAPTER TWENTY-SEVEN

THAT AFTERNOON, ADAM and Nick rode the horses. They followed the trail that led up the mountain from the back of the stables. Nick would usually ride each horse for about forty minutes in the morning and another forty in the afternoon. However, the men chose not to leave the women alone with Darren for so long, so they rode each horse for only fifteen minutes.

They had just returned and were feeding the stud when the motion sensors warned them that someone was approaching the ranch house and had already passed over the property line.

"It's on the main lane," Nick mentioned, after checking the tablet he still held in his pouch.

Without a word for Nick, Adam threw the hay from his fork in front of a hungry stallion. Then, he ran out of the stables toward the house. Still, he remembered to prop the fork on the wall by the door on his way out.

Nick shook his head but didn't follow Adam.

He knew that any intruder would need at least a quarter of an hour to get to the ranch house if they drove at full speed, and even more if they were on horses. So, he took the time to finish preparing his stud for the night.

When he came out of the stables, Nick closed the doors behind him and glanced toward the sky. The sun lay low in the west, and only a few puffy clouds floated above his head.

'*We won't have any rain tonight*,' the man judged with satisfaction, and then, he broke into a full run toward the cottage.

Nick only halted when he got to the front porch. There, his eyes laid on his friend, and he burst into laughter. Adam had already taken a defensive position behind a pillar on the veranda. Two rifles hung over his shoulders, and he held one in his hand.

"I see you're expecting an entire army," Nick teased his friend.

Adam scowled at him but didn't abandon his stance. "I don't see why you're laughing at me," Adam snapped at Nick. "We need to be ready. We've got two women in the house," he pointed out as if Nick forgot about Diane's and Darcy's presence.

Nick suddenly sobered and replied, "I haven't forgotten about the women in the house, Adam. However, I'm sure that the trespasser is Ryan. He said that they would be here around this time."

"And if it isn't Ryan? Then what?" Adam retorted, and his eyes sparkled with anger.

"Then, we'll do our best," Nick said in a quiet tone of voice and took out the two semi-automatic pistols he had shoved into his belt earlier.

"Good to know we're on the same page here," Adam mumbled grumpily.

"You know that I wouldn't let anything happen to Diane or Darcy," Nick said. "Besides, we handed a pistol to each girl before leaving the house," he thought to remind Adam.

"Huh!" Adam exclaimed. "As if that would do a lot of good. Diane doesn't believe in shooting people, and Darcy looks like a frightened rabbit," he said with mockery in his tone.

"She might look like that to you," Nick replied with annoyance. "Still, she's got guts. You should know that she crossed that mountain all by herself and at night," he pointed to the peaks visible in the distance beyond the cottage. "A scaredy-cat wouldn't do that," Nick concluded.

Adam shrugged but didn't take his eyes from the lane leading to the cottage. He knew that fear might push people to do things that they wouldn't usually think of doing, so his impression about Darcy didn't change a bit. He liked her, although he wouldn't have seen Nick fall for a woman like her.

Nick gave up convincing Adam and sighed. He stepped up onto the porch and leaned on the other pillar, gazing toward the lane, as well.

"And we've left them with Darren," Adam continued harping on Nick. "He might be wounded, but still, he could have seized a pistol from one of the women and taken them as hostages," he groused.

"Yes, he might have, but I have a feeling that the guy is all right. Have you seen anything untoward when you got into the house?" Nick asked Adam.

Adam shook his head with regret. He would have liked to flatten Darren, but the man hadn't given him a reason just yet.

"No, they are playing cards," Adam admitted. "I didn't tell them anything. I just went to get the rifles and came out here. But that doesn't mean that the guy is okay. He might play a role right now," he insisted in a stubborn tone of voice.

"He might," Nick agreed with him. "But, I doubt it."

Adam just waved his hand in disgust. Nick had really changed since the last time they met. He hadn't been so quick in believing in people before.

The sound of a car engine reached their ears before the car turned onto the lane, and Adam tensed, his finger on the trigger.

"Don't forget that it might be Ryan," Nick said in an indifferent tone of voice. "Maybe you won't shoot him."

"Funny," Adam growled but didn't take the finger off the trigger of his rifle.

A honk filled the ranch yard, and the car braked a couple of yards from the porch, the wheels sprawling pebbles everywhere. Ryan threw his door open, and his long legs appeared in view. The man stretched out and grinned at his friends.

"That's what I call a welcome," he laughed, and Nick's lips twitched.

Nick glanced at Adam. His friend had lowered the rifle, and now, he brushed his fingers through his hair.

Ryan shook his head and closed his car door. Then he went around the hood and helped Kate out.

"Come on, honey bun. The guys decided not to shoot us, after all," Ryan said maliciously, and his wife slapped his arm.

"Don't be mean, Ryan. They have reasons to be prudent," she pointed out.

Ryan just shrugged and slammed Kate's car door shut. Then he walked her up the stairs onto the porch. There, Nick caught Kate in a hug and crushed her to his chest.

"Hey, man, she's mine," Ryan pushed him away from his wife with a glower.

"Get used to that. Nick's like that now," Adam said to Ryan, waving his hand with disgust. "I don't know what got into him, but he's demonstrative like hell."

"I didn't know you saw me so cold and remote before," Nick observed in a dry tone of voice. "I thought that I always showed my feelings for all of you," he shifted his eyes from Kate to Ryan, and then to Adam.

"I've never thought you were cold," Kate patted his arm. "These two baboons have probably seen you like that because you weren't as vocal as they were," she explained to Nick and scowled at Adam and Ryan at the same time.

Adam rolled his eyes, and Ryan shrugged. Nick didn't comment. He merely nudged Kate into the house.

"Let's go inside. The girls are looking forward to seeing you," Nick said to Kate. "Even Darcy, although she has never met you before. But you know Diane. By now, she's told Darcy everything about you," he said with a broad smile on his lips.

"What do you mean?" Adam asked him in an upset tone of voice. "Do you want to say that Diane can't keep her mouth shut?"

"Mate, you're too sensitive," Nick shook his head. "I didn't mean any disrespect, man. I just said that Diane considered that Darcy should know a little about everybody. I actually appreciated her concern."

Adam didn't reply, but he narrowed his eyes to slits as if he thought that Nick only tried to sweeten the pot. Adam didn't buy it for a second.

CHAPTER TWENTY-EIGHT

DARCY AND DIANE WERE still playing cards with Darren when Kate came into the kitchen. They were so busy bickering that they didn't even notice Kate's arrival. Apparently, Darcy had won the third hand in a row, and the other two didn't seem convinced that she hadn't cheated.

Kate smiled and shook her head but decided to let them finish their squabble. She could wait for the guys to come before introducing herself to Darcy and Darren.

Nick, Adam, and Ryan had remained in the hallway near the front door to talk. Ryan asked Nick to tell him everything about what had happened before he offered sanctuary to Darren.

Adam had already informed Ryan about Nick's other guest. As Adam had expected, Ryan disliked the presence of an unknown man in the house.

"Are you sure that you've made the best decision?" Ryan asked Nick.

"I won't know for sure until the end," Nick confessed. "However, my instinct tells me that the guy is all right. I don't believe that we can rely on him if it comes to fighting, but I have no doubts that he isn't Driscoll's inside man," Nick reassured Ryan.

Ryan took a couple of seconds to reflect upon Nick's words and then said, "All right, then. I know that your instincts are sound, and I respect them."

"Be serious," Adam scoffed. "He might have had good instincts, but that was before he fell in love," the man waved his hand with disgust.

Nick narrowed his eyes and pressed his lips in a tight line. Adam had the unique talent to bring out the worse in everyone.

"Being in love doesn't automatically mean that I lost my mind, senses, or skills," Nick pointed out in a harsh tone of voice.

"So, you don't deny that you're in love," Adam exclaimed, and triumph sounded in his voice.

"Why would I?" Nick shrugged. "I know what I want and need. I don't need that someone else comes and points the obvious to me, like other people," he retorted. He wanted to remind Adam that he hadn't realized his love for Diane before Nick had told him.

"Huh! I might have been slow, but I had reasons," Adam snorted.

"Like what?" Ryan inquired, bracing his hands on his hips.

"My reasons," Adam mumbled. "I don't need to explain them to you," he replied stubbornly.

"Yeah, I can see that," Nick grinned. "Anyway, now that I confessed that I am in love, can we go to the kitchen? Or do you two intend to spend all evening here in the hall?"

"All right, we'll go," Ryan accepted with a brief nod. "However, we won't discuss any plans in front of Darren," he said in a flat tone of voice, staring sternly at Nick.

Nick nodded and said, "I haven't kept him apprised of my plans, either. I don't trust him so much anyway. We'll have dinner, and then I'll send him back to his bedroom. We can discuss our plans then."

"That's perfect," Ryan approved and waved to Adam to show him the way to the kitchen.

Adam saluted him mockingly and took the lead. When he got to the kitchen, he almost bumped into Kate, who was still listening to the lively argument between Darcy and the other two. Diane and Darren had banded against Darcy, but the young woman seemed to hold on her own just fine.

"What's going on?" Adam asked loudly with a frown and pushed by Kate, ready to intervene if Darren had done anything to Diane.

At his shout, the argument stopped, and the three-card players turned to the door. Darcy blushed when she noticed the audience, but Diane just laughed.

"You've come just in time. A little more and we would have come to blows," Diane joked, but Adam took her seriously and bad-mugged Darren.

"What did you do to her?"

The young man paled under Adam's enraged eyes, but Diane rose off her chair and came in front of Adam.

"Actually, Darren and I quarreled with Darcy. She seems to have some incredible luck at poker."

"It's not luck," Darcy intervened in a dry tone of voice. "It's science. I have been playing a lot with the grooms in the stables, and that for a few years already. Luck has nothing to do with that."

Nick grinned and started toward her. When he passed by Adam, he whispered, "A scared rabbit you said, hmm?"

Ryan grinned and shook his head. He liked seeing Nick like that. There had been moments when Ryan feared that Nick would never find someone, and that would have been a pity. Nick was quiet and rational, but he had a lot of generosity and felt deeply. He had a lot to give.

He watched Nick taking Darcy's hand and helping her up. He brought her to the group and introduced her to Kate first.

"This is Kate. I'm sure Diane told you a few things about her," he waved his fingers toward Kate.

Darcy smiled and shook Kate's hand. Indeed, Diane had told her quite a lot about Kate, and Darcy was a little intimidated. She knew that Kate could read her mind, and she was afraid of what the woman might see there.

Kate shook her head and reassured Darcy, "Don't worry. I don't pry if I don't have to. And besides, I like what I've just read in your mind. You're good for Nick."

Darcy blushed violently, and her fingers shook in Nick's hand. The man only squeezed her hand, reassuring her that everything was all right. Then he turned her to Ryan.

"This is my friend, Ryan. You've already heard his voice," he said, and lights danced in his eyes. Nick remembered well the last conversation he had had with Ryan and that Darcy heard.

Shyly, Darcy shook Ryan's hand, who beamed at her.

"I am delighted to meet you," Ryan said to her. "Nick needs someone in his life, and you seem to fit the bill."

"Ryan!" Kate exclaimed. "You always lack tact. You can't say something like that to people," she slapped him over his arm when she noticed that Darcy's blush intensified and reached the tips of her ears.

Diane and Adam just laughed. They already knew Ryan and didn't find anything weird in his words.

Nick sighed and pulled Darcy to him. "Don't pay any attention to him. You are in charge of your decisions. Nobody can tell you what to do," he said to her, staring meaningfully into her eyes. "Is it clear?"

Darcy nodded, but he could read uncertainty in her eyes. He leaned over her and whispered, "Regardless of everything, if you don't like me or don't want me, no one can push you into my direction, Darcy."

"It's not that," she whispered back. "It's just very sudden and unusual. It's not like I've felt this way before. I don't have any experience..."

"Then, it's good," Nick replied. "Take your time. I won't rush you," he promised in a severe tone of voice and squeezed Darcy's hand again.

"You know I can hear you," Adam whispered loudly. "And if I can, everyone can," he added teasingly.

"Damn, Adam, can't you shut up at least once?" Nick lost his temper and snapped at his friend.

Adam shrugged and said, "I was only saying. I thought you'd like to know that your efforts to whisper weren't successful. But I will shut up, no problem."

"Anyway, let's think of dinner people. We have a lot to talk afterward," Ryan intervened when Nick's eyebrows bunched on his forehead. The man seemed ready to jump at Adam's jugular.

"I vote for steaks," Adam hurried to say. "I took care to take some steaks out of Nick's freezer this afternoon. Let's bury your stew, Nick, and have a nice meal. Kate and Diane could make a nice potato salad..."

"It's fine by me," Nick shrugged. "The grill is in the back, though," he pointed to the door at the far end of the kitchen.

"Then, let's move people. The sun is setting. We're burning daylight here," Ryan ordered, and Kate's eyebrows rose.

"Really?" she inquired in a deceptively mild tone of voice.

"Come on, baby, let's move. I will help you peel the potatoes," Ryan tried to persuade her and putting his arm around her, he kissed her lips.

"All right, then," she accepted. "Let's do that. But Diane will keep company to Darcy. She needs her rest," Kate pointed out.

"I agree with you," Adam rushed to say, and taking his wife's hand, he pulled her after him to the back door.

CHAPTER TWENTY-NINE

DINNER TURNED INTO a boisterous affair. Everybody talked and laughed. Diane asked lots of questions about the twins, and Kate and Ryan regaled them with some of the kids' mischiefs.

"I'll turn white before my time," Ryan confessed, laughing. "Special Ops, guys? That's nothing, believe me. Try to raise twins. Thank God for Kate," he said, brushing his lips over his wife's fingers.

"She's got enough patience for both of us. I used to think that no one could make my blood pressure go up but Kate. Now, I know better."

Kate slapped him over the knee but laughed. Then she convinced the guys to share some stories from their special op days, and Darcy listened to everything wide-eyed. A couple of times, she even squeezed Nick's hand and cringed as if he were still in danger then.

Hearing about the guys' feats, Darren, who already was intimidated by the three men, looked at them in awe. Still, he started believing now that he had a chance to survive Driscoll's wrath if he had Nick, Adam, and Ryan on his side.

Dinner took so long that they had to put on the outside lights. Dark had already surrounded the backyard by the time they finished their steaks and potato salad.

Adam couldn't refrain from commenting about Kate's and Diane's culinary talents, and Darcy felt out of place. Nick reassured Darcy that cooking wasn't everything, and she certainly had other skills that were equally valuable, if not more.

"I, for one, don't care if you can't boil an egg," he said to her, and he believed that indeed.

"Amen to that," Ryan approved, and rose, starting to clear up the table.

The others followed his suit and brought the dishes to the kitchen. However, for about an hour afterward, they still lingered outside, everyone drinking beer, except Darcy and Diane, who asked for soft drinks.

"We should discuss our plans," Ryan said when a break appeared in the conversation. He looked pointedly at Darren, and the man stood up immediately.

"I'll go to my room," Darren announced, understanding that the men didn't want to discuss their plans with him. He didn't mind because he wouldn't have done it either if he were in their place.

Everyone wished him *good night*, and Nick added, "There are some magazines and books in the living room if you're interested. You know, to pass the time."

Darren shook his head, though, and said, "I'm tired. I think I'll go directly to bed."

"All right then, we'll see you tomorrow," Nick nodded, and Darren left.

Nick waited until the man disappeared inside the house and then said, "We should go back into the kitchen, though. Darren might hear what we're talking about if we remain here. His window overlooks the backyard," he explained.

"All right then," Ryan said. He began picking up the empty bottles. "Let's go."

Everyone followed him, and once they brought everything back into the kitchen, Diane said, "I'll do the dishes, guys."

Darcy shook her head immediately. "No, you should rest. I'll do the dishes."

"No, sweetie," Nick shook his head at his turn. "You should rest as well. I'll take care of everything," he reassured her.

Nonplussed, Darcy stared at him and braced her hands on her hips. For a few seconds, she wasn't able to say anything.

"Are you serious?" she finally managed to push the words past her lips. "I did nothing all day long while you took care of your devices and the horses. If anyone should rest, it is you."

Nick stubbornly contradicted her and shook his head once more. Adam, who was watching the exchange between Darcy and Nick with curiosity, threw his hands in the air.

"Is everyone okay if I do the dishes?" he inquired with exasperation, and Ryan burst into laughter.

"Be my guest. Just hurry because we need your input as well," Ryan said with a negligent wave of his hand and then took a seat at the table.

Kate looked around undecided. Adam had already started doing the dishes under Darcy's wide eyes.

Diane just shrugged and joined Ryan at the table. Nick came to Darcy, and taking her hand, he steered her toward the table.

"Adam will do just fine, don't worry," he whispered to her, helping her to take a seat.

"You know I'm not made of porcelain, and I won't break," Darcy inquired in a huff.

"Of course, you aren't," Nick approved. "Still, you've gone through a lot these last few days, and I want you not to worry about anything," he insisted.

"You can't shelter her from everything," Kate interjected, taking a seat in the chair next to Ryan.

"You might want to, but it's not possible. Tell him, Ryan. You know how it is," she nudged her husband.

"I know, baby. But that doesn't mean that I don't want to keep you safe all the time. Nick's the same. I understand."

Kate rolled her eyes and shrugged. She turned to Darcy and told her, "That's how these macho guys are. I'm sorry, sweetie, but you chose him. Now you have to deal with his personality, as well. Right, Diane?" she turned to the other woman.

"Tell me about it!" Diane exclaimed.

"What do you mean?" Adam turned from the sink, a frown on his face.

Suds fell off his hands on the floor, and Nick looked pointedly at the spotted boards, but Adam didn't care. He just stared at Diane, waiting for her answer.

"Only that sometimes you nag me like an old woman," Diane replied with a shrug.

"Like when?" Adam inquired, and his stern eyes stared at her.

"Like on the way here," Diane replied. "You kept telling me to keep close to your side and not to venture outside or try to do anything."

"But that's for your own good. You're pregnant, woman. And we're not on vacation here," Adam lost his calm and shouted.

"And do you think I didn't understand that from the get-go?" Diane rose an eyebrow.

"If you had understood, you wouldn't have come with me. You'd have stayed at home, where you would have been safe," the man raised his voice again.

"Would you have some care with my boards?" Nick inquired. "If you can't do the dishes, just say so."

"I'm talking to my wife," Adam turned to Nick like a bull challenged to fight.

"Children," Ryan rose. He raised his hands and claimed everyone's attention.

"I think we should calm down. Adam, take care of those dishes. Girls, you have to understand that we'll always worry, and yes, we'll nag. It's in our nature. Case closed. Nick, I'm sure your wood boards wouldn't get ruined because of some suds," Ryan pointed out.

Adam threw another bleak look to his wife and returned to the sink. Ryan strode to the fridge and took a few bottles out to bring to the table.

Then he sat down, satisfied that no one had any more comments.

CHAPTER THIRTY

THE MEN PATROLLED NICK'S territory systematically, as they had planned the night before. At the same time, they also helped Nick with his horses because he still needed to ride them. Ryan had agreed that they could reach some particular areas better on horseback than by car.

Initially, Ryan thought of taking the women with them as well, but Adam had firmly vetoed that plan. He didn't believe that Diane should be on a horse in her situation.

Diane hadn't contradicted him. She knew that she couldn't change Adam's mind when he went into protective mode. The stubborn setting of his chin and the hardness in his eyes didn't invite to negotiations.

Kate and Darcy had refused going riding with the men. They didn't want to leave Diane alone with Darren in the cottage. However, Kate had already reassured first Ryan and then the others that Darren didn't have any wicked plans in mind. Still, Kate had insisted that three women had more chances than only one if anything had happened.

In the end, all the women had remained at home. They promised to have a good lunch at the ready at around one o'clock. Kate and Diane knew their way in the kitchen, so

Adam had sighed with relief. He understood that he didn't have to make do with Nick's food again. Adam didn't think his stomach would agree with another of Nick's experiments.

The men were riding the last lot of horses back home when a high pitch came from Nick's tablet and warned them that someone had trespassed the property line. Nick took the iPad out from the pouch to verify the intruders' position and frowned.

"Where?" Ryan asked, his face darkened. He suspected that Nick didn't have good news.

"Three spots, damn it," Nick growled. "This time, Driscoll must have brought reinforcements," he groused through locked teeth.

Adam swore a blue stream and reined his horse intending to throw him into a gallop, but Ryan stopped him.

"Only fools rush in," he warned his friend in a hard tone of voice.

"The women are alone, man," Adam retorted furiously.

"And we'll do a lot of good if we jump into the fray without thinking," Ryan replied in a calm tone of voice.

"Anyway, we have to go now," Nick intervened. "They are close to the cottage. We still have to ride up that hill and then down," he pointed in the distance.

"I vote that we go now," Adam decided. "You can think of a plan on our way there," he told Ryan and urged his mount into a sprint.

Ryan shook his head, staring after his anxious friend. He understood Adam's concerns. Ryan worried as well, but he always believed that a good plan made the difference between defeat and victory. The man sighed deeply and then signaled for Nick to follow him.

The two men took their horses into a canter to catch up with Adam. They had been together for a long time. Ryan and Nick knew that their friend was inclined to act first and think after. No one said a word during their ride back home. Adam and Nick turned various scenarios into their heads while Ryan built a strategy.

A few minutes before getting out of the forest, gunshots in close succession reached their ears. Adam roared his anguish and pushed his mount faster.

Ryan shouted after him, "Adam, go to the back door."

Adam just waved his hand above his head to show that he had heard Ryan's words but didn't stop.

"Don't forget to take the two semiautomatic pistols I duct-taped underneath the picnic table last night. You might need more firepower than you have on you," Ryan advised his friend with another shout and then sighed. He wasn't sure if Adam had heard him. The man was incensed to get to the house and had already lengthened the horse's stride.

"I didn't have time to remind him about the four pairs of handcuffs and the knives," Ryan groused, full of disappointment.

"He remembers about them, don't worry," Nick said quietly. "I suppose I'll go inside through the front door, and you'll take the cellar."

Ryan merely nodded and pushed his horse harder. His features didn't show the anxiety he felt, but every fiber in his body was in knots.

'*Damn it! One of us should have stayed behind. So stupid not to think that they might attack in broad daylight,*' he scolded himself.

Ryan glanced at Nick sideways and sighed inwardly. He noticed the tight line of Nick's lips. A muscle twitched in the man's jaw, and his knuckles had already whitened on the reins.

CHAPTER THIRTY-ONE

ADAM YANKED THE TWO semiautomatic pistols from under the picnic table. Then he hurried with quiet steps to the back door, which laid wide open.

'*Amateurs,*' he thought. '*They haven't left anyone outside.*'

The man leaned on the jamb and tilted his head to look inside the kitchen. A body was lying on the floor in front of the sink. It was definitely a man, so Adam didn't care about him.

A man with sandy hair came to his fallen comrade and helped him to sit up in spite of his groans. Blood ran freely from one of the wounded man's thighs.

"Can you walk?" the sandy-haired man asked his buddy, but this one shook his head and groaned. "Damn, I'll have to carry you out," the man grumbled and pulled him up, draping him over his shoulders afterward.

Weighed down by the injured man's body, the sandy-haired man shuffled his feet toward the back door. When he got out, Adam pushed a cocked pistol under his nose.

The man's eyes widened, and his lips parted in surprise.

He needed a moment to realize what was happening. Then he wanted to warn the others in the house, so he drew air into his lungs to shout out, but Adam shook his head.

"I wouldn't do it if I were you," he advised the man. "Just put your friend there," Adam tilted his head toward the side of the house. "Then kneel with your hands at the back of your head, facing the wall," he ordered harshly.

The man tried to judge his chances, and an ugly grin appeared on Adam's lips. He understood what thoughts crossed the man's mind.

He waved one of his pistols toward the guy and said, "Yeah, you can try to attack me, but I'll still fire the gun I have in my right hand. As you can see, the target is your belly. Well, the choice is yours," Adam added and shrugged with indifference.

Adam wouldn't have liked to shoot the man and divulge his position but considered that he would handle the situation if necessary.

The man decided that it wasn't worth dying stupidly for Driscoll. He let the injured man slide down next to the wall of the cottage. Then, he knelt on the ground, putting his hands on the back of his head.

Adam kept his eyes and pistol trained on the two men while he stepped carefully back toward the picnic table. He snatched two of the pairs of handcuffs that Ryan had duct-taped to the table and then returned to his two hostages.

With the barrel of his pistol, Adam tapped on the shoulder of the man kneeling on the ground.

"With your right hand, take your friend's right hand."

"Can I turn around?" the man asked.

"What would be the point then?" Adam retorted. "No, keep kneeling and take the man's right hand. Then lift both hands into the air," he ordered.

The man obeyed, so Adam handcuffed them quickly and stepped back out of the man's reach.

"Now, join your left hands and lift them in the air," Adam asked. After he put the handcuffs on their left wrists, Adam inquired, "How many of you came?"

"We're twenty-two, Driscoll included."

"Now, that's good," Adam approved. "That Driscoll's also here, I mean, because I don't like it that you came. Anyway, what happened to the women?" Adam asked in such a hard tone of voice that the man cringed.

"One shot my cousin here," he said, pointing his chin to the wounded man. "The redhead," he specified. "She was still shooting when I went to help my cousin."

"Good for her," Adam said, proud of his wife. "Was she hurt?" he asked.

"I don't know," the man shrugged. "I saw Gabe rush to her, though. He's a nasty one. She might not have made it."

Adam saw red before his eyes and gritted his teeth. His feet were itching to run into the kitchen and see what happened to Diane.

"You weren't very helpful, pal," he growled. "You need to sleep for a while so that I know for sure that you don't move," he added and knocked the man with the gun handle over the head.

The man fell over his cousin with a faint groan. Adam watched him with satisfaction and then approached the kitchen door again. Shots still rang inside the room, but now, sounds of gunfire came from other sides of the house as well.

He entered the kitchen with the pistols at the ready and shot the first man he noticed. The bullet went directly through the hand that was holding a gun.

The man screamed, and the weapon fell off his fingers. Instead of attacking Adam, the man ran out of the kitchen, squealing.

Another guy turned toward Adam and fired at him, but his target was far off, and he shot Nick's stew pot.

Adam grinned. '*Not a big waste. Thank God, I won't have to eat that food again.*' Then, Adam returned the favor with two bullets, one through the man's hand and one through his leg. With a yelp, the man fell to the floor like a log. '*This one doesn't howl at least,*' Adam reflected.

The kitchen floor was literally littered with bodies. Besides the men Adam had shot, four others lay on the wooden boards spotted with blood. '*Nick will have a fit when he sees those boards,*' Adam thought and shrugged.

The door to the cellar opened, and Adam took a position to shoot. Luckily, he recognized Ryan's checkered flannel shirt and stopped in time.

"Welcome to the party," Adam said dryly. "Now, we only have to find the women."

"Yeah, we should. But let check these people here first," Ryan said. "We must make sure that we won't be ambushed afterward. We need to tie up everyone who's still moving," he explained, taking a coil of rope he had brought from the cellar.

Adam grimaced but saw the reason for his friend's proposition. He took out the knife he had shoved into his belt and cut a few lengths of rope from Ryan's coil to tie the guy he had shot and who was still crying holding his hand. A blow well-aimed at the man's temple quieted him, and then, Adam tied his hands together.

"Adam, come here," Ryan's voice reached Adam's ears when he was standing up.

Adam turned to Ryan and saw him rolling over a big guy with an ugly mug. Then, Adam noticed his wife's lifeless body and fairly growled running toward her.

"Don't tell me she's dead," he roared at Ryan before reaching his wife.

"Calm down, Adam. She isn't. I think that this immense guy fell on top of her and knocked the wind out of her sails. Diane's still breathing. Most of the blood on her clothes isn't hers, I guarantee. You check Diane, and I will take care of the others," Ryan proposed, putting a reassuring hand on Adam's shoulder.

Adam just nodded and brushed his fingers over Diane's delicate neck. He felt the pulse beating steadily under the tips of his fingers and sighed with relief. He could deal with everything else, but not with her death.

"I'll chain you to the bed from now on if you still want to come with me on such trips," he mumbled gruffly when his eyes fell on a bruise the size of a man's fist on her jaw.

"No, really?" Diane whispered, and her eyelids fluttered for a few moments. When she opened her eyes, her pupils shone with pain, and Adam gnashed his teeth.

"You're lucky that you're already battered," Adam said. "Otherwise, I'd spank you right now for putting me through all of this."

"Good to know that you think of what I put you through," Diane replied in a huff. "I'd have thought you'd consider what I went through."

"Of course, I am, baby," Adam whispered and stroked the side of her face. Unshed tears sparkled in his eyes. "Where are you hurt?"

"Just the jaw," Diane replied, and her fingers intertwined with Adam's. "That huge man hit me with his fist after I shot him the first time, but I think I shot him a second time before I blacked out. He fell on me, probably."

Adam nodded and brushed the hair off her face. He leaned over her and kissed her. "Do you hurt anywhere else?"

Diane nodded and licked her lips. She touched her ribs with her other hand and then said, "I think everything hurts right now. The was a giant, really. But I don't think that anything happened to the baby," she rushed to assure Adam.

"We'll see a doctor soon," he promised to her. "Don't worry about anything."

CHAPTER THIRTY-TWO

RYAN FINISHED BINDING everyone's hands quickly and returned to Diane's side, although his mind lay somewhere else.

'*Where the hell are you, Kate? I'm going to strangle you, woman. You had to come. You couldn't have stayed at home where you were safe and sound,*' he ground his teeth.

"Is everything all right here?" Ryan asked in a tense tone of voice when he reached Diane and Adam. At the same time, his eyes swept all over the woman's body to see if she had any wounds anywhere.

Diane nodded slightly because her head hurt, and then, she stroked Ryan's hand to reassure him. She read well the tension in the man's eyes and suspected that his mind was actually on Kate's whereabouts and well-being.

"Darren helped Kate and Darcy run out of the kitchen and up the stairs," Diane said to Adam and Ryan, and she licked her dry lips again. "I was too far away though, and he couldn't reach me," she added.

"He tried," she said in a stronger tone of voice when she noticed Adam's scowl. "I asked them to go. I knew you would come, guys. I thought it would be easier for you to free only one person instead of three," she explained her reasons.

In spite of her explanations, Adam's brows bunched on his forehead, and his eyes turned harder. Reluctantly, Adam agreed with Diane, but still, he didn't like that his wife was left behind.

Suddenly the sound of gunshots ceased in the cottage, and an eerie silence descended over them. All three of them exchanged a look, and then they turned their eyes to the door that led toward the rest of the house as if the answer for the sudden lack of noises laid there.

When that silence stretched for more minutes, Ryan stood with impatience and said, "I'm going out and see what's going on."

"No need," Nick's hard voice came from the door. "I finished all of them, more or less. I think I killed two of them, though. I couldn't stop them otherwise. Unfortunately, Driscoll isn't one of the two," Nick remarked with regret. "He looks like he'll survive, although with a permanent limp," Nick continued and shrugged with indifference. He didn't care one way or another about Driscoll's future, but he rejoiced knowing that the man wouldn't harm anyone in the future.

Nick shoved the pistol he had in his hand into the waistband of his pants and brushed his fingers through his hair.

His friends watched him with apprehension. They didn't like the grim light in Nick's eyes. They knew that he had something more to say, and besides, he didn't have Darcy and Kate with him.

"I don't know about Darren yet, though. He's been shot at least three times," Nick shook his head. "I found him on the floor in front of my bedroom. He's bleeding like a stabbed pig," the man explained with a scowl on his face.

"And the women?" Ryan asked with anxiety. He couldn't stand the suspense anymore, although he was also afraid of Nick's answer.

"Darcy must have remembered the way to my secret passage," Nick replied to Ryan and then wiped the sweat off his forehead with his sleeve. "They're nowhere else in the house," he explained. "I've also noticed some drops of blood in front of the wardrobe in my bedroom, so one of them is hurt," the man concluded.

Nick clenched and unclenched his fists for a couple of seconds to release his tension, but it didn't work. Anger raged freely inside him, and he had a hard time to look into Ryan's eyes.

He knew that his friend's heart must have been in knots at the news of Kate's missing.

Nick flexed his shoulders and continued, "I'm going after them now. Adam, you should help with binding all the men upstairs because I didn't have enough rope with me to tie all of them. They are all incapacitated in a way or another but.... Anyway, I believe we'd better restrain them. I also think that Ryan should call Mark and talk to him. We'll have to call the sheriff and probably, an ambulance or something," Nick shook his head. "There's no way around that, guys. We've got wounded and dead all over the cottage. But let's see what Mark says first," Nick said with a shrug.

Ryan hesitated for a second. He would have liked to go after Kate and see that she was all right, but he understood that Nick knew the passage better, so he should go and take care of the women.

"All right, Nick. You go after them. We'll take care of the rest."

CHAPTER THIRTY-THREE

NICK LEFT ADAM TO TAKE care of restraining the men on the first floor, and he went to take a flashlight from a drawer. The man doubted that Darcy and Kate had the time to bring a lamp with them. Then he opened the panel to the secret passage.

Nick descended the stairs with quick footsteps. His jaw clenched harder at the sight of blood smeared on the wall, and the blood drops on the steps.

He reached the fork in the corridor and chose to follow the path to the shelter. Darcy didn't know what she could find if she went the other way, and he didn't see her risking getting lost or caught, mainly because either she or Kate was hurt.

Nick reached the entrance to the shelter, and his heart started beating faster. He was scared of what would wait for him behind that door.

The man couldn't stand the thought of Darcy's being hurt, but he didn't know how he would face Ryan either if Kate had been the one wounded.

Nick knocked on the door with his fist and shouted, "Darcy, Kate, it's me, Nick. Open up."

He had insulated that room well, so he couldn't hear what happened inside, although he listened attentively. Nick's anxiety increased tenfold.

A few muffled noises reached his ears, but the door still didn't open. Nick knocked again and harder until his knuckles started to bleed.

Suddenly, the door opened, and Nick barely stopped not to hit Kate with his fist. Kate's face was pale, and her eyes were red, sign that she had cried.

Blood traces covered Kate's entire left arm, and Nick sighed deeply. The woman had torn a strip from her t-shirt and bound it around her biceps.

Nick scowled and shook his head. He brushed the side of the woman's face with the tips of his fingers and said, "I'm really sorry, Kate. You shouldn't have been hurt."

"It's not your fault, Nick," she patted his arm reassuringly. "You didn't shoot me, after all."

"Still, Ryan will have my head," Nick tried to joke, but his attempt sounded lame even in his ears.

Kate waved his concerns away with her hand and then invited him to enter with another broad gesture. She also took the flashlight from Nick and shoved into her back pocket. She knew that he would need to have both hands free.

"Darcy's not well at all, Nick, and she needs to see a doctor urgently," Kate said with regret in her voice. "Someone shot her in her left side and right thigh. The bullets went through, and I think that's good. Still, she is very pale and had lost a lot of blood," Kate warned him.

Nick's heart skipped a beat, and the man fairly growled. He pushed by Kate impatiently and strode toward the cot he had previously set in the corner of the room.

Darcy laid on the cot utterly spent. Her eyelashes fluttered at the sound of Nick's steps on the cement floor. With effort, she opened her eyes and turned her head toward him.

Nick practically stumbled at the sight of Darcy's white face and lips. Even the cobalt of her irises had paled. Nick couldn't refrain himself anymore and swore bitterly, clasping his fists.

Darcy winced, and Nick closed the distance between them immediately. He knelt next to the woman and touched her lightly, afraid not to jolt her and make her suffer more than she did.

"Oh, sweetie, I'm so damn sorry," he whispered and touched his forehead to Darcy's head. "I should have been there and protect you," he said, and pain colored his tone of voice.

"Don't be silly, Nick," Darcy replied in a weak voice and tried to reach his hand. "You haven't done anything else but protect me so far."

Nick noticed Darcy's attempt to take his hand. He realized that she didn't have enough energy left to complete the gesture, so he intertwined his fingers with hers. He lifted her hand carefully to his mouth, and his lips brushed with tenderness over her knuckles.

"I must take you out of here, baby," he whispered again. "We must go back to the house. Ryan said that he would call for medical help, so someone will take a look at your wounds soon. I know that you'd prefer to lie down, and I might hurt you while I am carrying you up the stairs, but I can't leave you here, Darcy," Nick explained to her in a voice filled with regret and sorrow.

"I know, Nick, don't worry. I'll be fine," Darcy replied and flexed her fingers in Nick's hand.

"All right, sweetie," Nick approved of her determination. "Could you put your arms around my neck?"

Darcy looked doubtful but tried. After two failed attempts, she slid her arms around Nick's neck with his help, and she knotted her fingers in his shirt.

"That's my girl," Nick praised her with a shadow of a smile on his lips. He eased an arm underneath her legs and the other around her back, and then rose, gathering the woman to his chest.

A faint moan flew off Darcy's lips, and the woman sagged against him. Nick's mouth turned into a thin line. A sickening feeling filled his chest, and he tightened his teeth so that he wouldn't roar his fury.

Careful not to jar Darcy, Nick turned toward the door, and his eyes fell on Kate. The woman was leaning on the wall next to the door. He stopped brusquely, and his eyes swept over Kate's body attentively.

"Can you climb the stairs, or do you need help?" he asked Kate softly.

Kate straightened and shook her head. She took out the flashlight she had stuffed in the pocket of her jeans and turned it on. Then, she put out the light in the shelter and started before Nick toward the stairs.

CHAPTER THIRTY-FOUR

THE CELL PHONE FELL off Ryan's hand when the man set eyes on his wife. He saw red before his eyes and bit his lower lip not to shout at her. He was aware that Kate hadn't chosen to stand before a bullet. However, she had insisted on coming with him, although she knew that risks would arouse.

'I'll yell at you later when you don't look so run down. Oh, yes, sweetie, I'll make your ears burn,' he promised to himself, and his eyes narrowed.

Forgetting about the cell phone and Mark, who kept asking what was going on, Ryan strode toward Kate with purposeful steps. He didn't dare to touch her injured arm but asked in a strained tone of voice, "Are you hurt anywhere else?"

The woman shook her head, and the next second, Ryan's arm slid behind her, and he crushed her to his chest forcefully. She yelped, but the man didn't hear anything. Ryan buried his head in Kate's honey-colored hair and clung to her as if he were on the verge of losing her.

"It's just a scratch, Ryan," she patted him on the back. "It has even stopped bleeding," she told him with conviction.

"A scratch?" Ryan shouted, drawing back and staring at Kate with bewilderment. "Are you out of your mind, woman? Do you want me to age before my time? I'll take you home and lock you in the house so that you couldn't get into such situations anymore," Ryan continued roaring. He forgot about his promise not to shout at her right then.

Kate grimaced and said, "You're exaggerating now." Then, she patted his arm and reassured him, "You'll forget about it in no time."

"Are you making fun of me?" Ryan's eyes popped out of his head. "Forget about you being shot?"

"Don't get dramatic. It's not the end of the world. I'll be fine in a day or two," Kate said with nonchalance.

"Kate, listen here and listen good," Ryan started to say, but Diane interrupted him.

"Where's Darcy?" she asked.

Both Kate and Ryan turned to her. Adam had carried Diane to one of the kitchen chairs when she refused to lie down on the sofa in the living room, and from there, she watched them with curiosity.

"Nick decided that she should wait in bed until medical help comes. Unfortunately, she's been wounded badly," Kate replied with sadness.

Diane's lips parted, and she sighed softly. "Oh, my," she whispered. "That's bad."

"Yes, it is," Kate concurred with Diane's evaluation. "Still, I hope that Darcy will heal," Kate bit her lips, and then she covered her midriff with her sound arm. "Where's Adam?" she inquired.

"He's doing a tour around the house and the barn," Ryan informed her in a dry tone of voice. "I'm going to talk to Nick," he decided and turned to go out of the kitchen. "You both are safe. There's no attacker free in the house."

"You forgot your cell phone," Diane tilted her head to the phone on the floor.

Only then, Ryan realized that Mark was still speaking, asking them what was going on.

"Damn," Ryan cursed and bent to take the phone. "Yeah, I'm still here, Mark. We need more than one ambulance, and soon. Nick's girlfriend is hurt badly," he informed Mark on his way toward the stairs.

Ryan found Nick in the bedroom. On his knees next to the bed, Nick held one of Darcy's hands in his. He stared at her intently as if he could make her recover only with the power of his mind.

"Hey, brother," Ryan said softly. "How is she?" he asked Nick.

Nick shrugged impotently and shook his head.

"Have you looked at her injuries?" Ryan insisted. He didn't like his friend's prostration and wanted to jar him into action.

Nick nodded, and this time, he replied in a huff, turning his angry eyes to Ryan, "Of course, I have. The bleeding stopped. Both wounds are flesh injuries. However, she lost a lot of blood."

"Mark sent the emergency services here," Ryan said and approached the other side of the bed. He leaned over Darcy and checked her pulse. "It's a bit weak, but she'll make it, Nick."

"Are you a doctor?" Nick narrowed his eyes and threw a black glance at his friend.

"You're too worried right now to know better," Ryan shook his head. "You need to take a step back and get detached a little. Then, you'd see that I was right."

Nick jumped up with pent-up fury. "Detached, you say?"

"Cool off, brother," Ryan tried to stop his friend's anger. "I know you can't. But I'm telling you that she'll make it."

Nick growled, but Darcy's soft whisper stopped him. "Nick, please, don't worry so much. I'll be fine."

The man forgot about Ryan in an instant and dropped next to Darcy again. "How are you feeling, baby?" he asked her in an anxious voice. Darcy hadn't said a word since he took her out of the shelter.

"Honestly, I've been better," she grimaced. "But I don't think I'm going to die," she attempted to chase away Nick's concerns.

"I've never thought you would die, sweetie," Nick replied gruffly. "I love you, and you can't leave me now," he said without thinking.

"No worries, Nick. I love you too. I have only found you, so I can't leave you now. I need time with you," Darcy smiled at Nick, and her fingers tightened on his.

Nick stroked her face, and in the spur of the moment, he leaned over her and kissed her lips.

"Ryan says that the ambulance is coming," he straightened and said, glancing at Ryan, who nodded reassuringly.

"So, you don't have to worry," Darcy flexed her fingers in Nick's hand. "I'll be fine in no time. You'll see," she practically promised to him and closed her eyes once more. Her hand sagged in Nick's hands, and he squeezed it as if he had wanted to give her some of his strength.

Nick watched her chest rising and falling and ground his teeth with impotent rage. After a few seconds, he looked up at Ryan. His eyes met the man's impenetrable glance, and Nick's expression turned grimmer.

CHAPTER THIRTY-FIVE

"YOUR FRIENDS HAVE ARRIVED," a young nurse whispered in Nick's ear, and the man rose.

He had been sitting and watching Darcy for the last few hours. Nick hadn't moved from the chair set next to her bed since the emergency doctor finished patching Darcy, and the nurses moved her to a private room.

Nick thanked the nurse, and with a last glance at Darcy, who was sleeping fitfully, he went out and strode toward the waiting room. Besides his friends, he noticed only another small group of three people in there, gathered in the corner of the room. They talked among themselves and didn't pay any attention to the newcomer.

Diane saw Nick come into the room and rushed to hug him. "How are you holding?" she asked him with concern.

He smiled faintly at the redhead and shrugged.

"I'm fine, Diane. Darcy seems to recover. However, the doctor said that it would be a few days before I can take her out of the hospital," he explained ruefully.

Then, he brushed his fingers through his hair with a nervous gesture.

"So Darcy will recover, Nick. That's important," Adam thumped Nick over the shoulder without restraint, and Nick grimaced.

"We'll wait for her to come out of the hospital, Nick," Kate reassured him. "The guys will take care of your stud, so you shouldn't worry about anything."

Ryan and Adam nodded, approving of her words, and Nick thanked them.

"I'm sorry for all the trouble, guys. I can't leave her alone here. I know you understand."

"Don't trouble yourself, Nick," Ryan put his hand on Nick's shoulder. "Of course, we understand. We can stay at least a couple of weeks. If we need to stay longer, Mark will send the kids here by plane."

"And we have a guy who takes care of our ranch regularly," Adam mentioned. "So, it isn't a big deal if we spend some more time with you here, mate. I'm actually happy because Diane will have the time to recover fully as well."

Nick didn't have the opportunity to answer to Adam because the same nurse who had announced him about his friends' presence in the waiting room came to talk to him again.

"Sir, a couple has arrived just now. The woman insists on checking Darcy out of the hospital and taking her somewhere else. She claims to be her mother."

Nick's eyes narrowed to slits. He tensed and clenched his fists, then he rushed out of the waiting room. His pals followed him immediately.

PULLED IN

The nurse at the reception desk argued with a forty-something-old woman and a middle-aged man, whom Nick recognized immediately. On several occasions, he had seen the older man together with Driscoll in town.

"What's the problem here?" Nick asked in a hard tone of voice.

The couple turned to him, and the woman stared at him with venom in her eyes. "None of your business, mister," she replied to Nick peevishly. "Move along. This is a private matter," she waved her hand dismissively.

"I'm afraid it is my business," Nick retorted, staring the woman down.

"Not where my daughter is involved. You are just nobody. I have the right to decide about my daughter's care, and I decided that she would come with me," Wanda Burnett snapped at him, thundering him with her eyes.

"Darcy's over eighteen, so you don't have any saying in her medical care anymore. I'm her fiancée and future husband. I decide the kind of care she gets until she can make that decision by herself," Nick replied in a resolute tone of voice, refusing to back down before the woman.

Wanda looked at him wide-eyed, but she recovered soon and snorted. "Huh! You're out of your mind, cowboy. She'll marry Driscoll. You're nobody, as I've already said," she smirked at him.

Adam intervened with an ugly grin on his face. "Everything else aside, I really don't see the point to insist on marrying her to a man who will spend a few decades in prison," he pointed out.

Wanda Burnett turned to Adam with a black look. She measured the man from the top of his head to the bottom of his feet. Appreciation sparkled in her eyes, but she recovered soon.

"You don't know what you are talking about," she dismissed Adam as well. "Emmett won't go to prison because he didn't do anything wrong, and Darcy will testify to that. I'll see to it. Anyway, what can anyone expect from white trash like you?" the woman said with scorn and snorted again.

"Just call him white trash once more," Diane's angry voice interfered.

The young woman stepped closer to Wanda, her body vibrating with anger. "I'll take your eyes out, you two-time piece of shit," she barked.

Everyone stared at Diane with astonishment, although with different reasons. Most of them had never expected to hear such words coming out of the woman's mouth.

Only Adam grinned happily and said, "That's my girl." He grabbed Diane by the waist and pulled her to him. Then he kissed her mouth hard, making the younger nurse blush.

Ryan put his thumb in the air, congratulating Adam for appreciating his wife's wit.

"I think your business here has just ended," Nick informed Wanda in a cold tone of voice and turned to go back to Darcy's private hospital room.

"Not so fast," Darcy's mother stopped him and then turned to the nurse at the reception desk. "I will sue this hospital to the high sky. I'm a first-degree relative, and I have the right to see my daughter and make decisions on her behalf. He has no claim over Darcy," she pointed toward Nick.

"I think that you should keep the money for your own trial," a cold male voice intervened.

The woman gasped and turned to the new intruder. A lanky six-feet tall man returned her look with disdain. His pale green eyes froze Wanda Burnett to the core.

"Hey, man," Ryan shook the man's hand. "I didn't know you were on your way here."

"I wouldn't have missed this trip for nothing in the world. I wanted to make sure that everything turns out well with Nick," the man brushed his fingers through his disheveled curly coppery hair.

"Don't worry, Kate," he turned his eyes to Ryan's wife. "The kids are fine. Jeanne is with them. I also left a team of three agents with them. Those women are my best female agents, and all of them are mothers, so they have experience with children. I didn't think that Jeanne would survive by herself," he shook his head. "Man, you don't have kids," he said to Ryan with exasperation, raising his hands. "They're terrorists, not children, believe me. One more day and I'd have fallen into pieces."

Kate blushed because she knew that the kids speculated the people's slightest weakness, which they had probably done with Mark. Ryan laughed heartily and thumped Mark over the shoulder.

"Very touching," Wanda's dry voice interrupted their discussion. "Still, I want to see my daughter and take her out of here."

"Not so fast, Ms. Burnett," Mark stopped her with an authoritative gesture. "You and your friend are under arrest for human trafficking and home invasion. There are a few more charges, but for the moment, these will suffice," he shrugged, and turning toward the entrance of the hospital aisle, he waved to a few people to come forward. Six agents strode onto the corridor, their handcuffs at the ready.

"You have no authority to arrest me," Wanda shrieked and stepped back.

"Personally, no. However, I have the mandates here, and these guys are police officers from the Human Trafficking Taskforce. I'm afraid that they do have the authority to arrest you and remove you off the hospital premises," Mark said in a dry tone of voice. Then he signaled the officers to take the two people in custody.

Wanda vociferated loudly, and a few heads appeared out of the nearby rooms. However, the officers led the woman and her companion toward the exit efficiently. The nurses reassured the patients that everything was in order, and they could return to their rooms.

Nick turned to his friends and said, "I'm going back to Darcy. I want to be there when she wakes up," he explained.

"Of course, you do," Kate exclaimed. "We'll go back to the cottage and wait for your call. Is it okay?" she inquired.

"Yes, please," Nick said. "Thank you, Mark," he turned to his former boss. "Your intervention was perfectly timed," Nick admitted. He knew that the nurses would have had to let Wanda go to her daughter's room if the agents hadn't removed her.

"Don't mention it, man. Just take care of yourself and your woman," Mark bumped his fist with Nick's.

Nick nodded and started back to Darcy's room. His friends followed him by sight. When Nick closed the door behind him, Ryan turned to Mark.

"Do you have to leave now, or can you spare a few hours to visit with us, at least?"

"I can spare even a few days," Mark shrugged. "I have to stay anyway. I want to make sure that the guys from the human trafficking task force don't let anyone slip away. I suppose Nick has a sofa for me. I'd prefer to stay with you instead of going to a hotel," Mark pointed out.

"You suppose correctly," Adam told him and slapped him over the shoulder. Then, he slid his arm around his wife's waist and started toward the exit.

CHAPTER THIRTY-SIX

SEVERAL DAYS PASSED until Nick returned with Darcy back to the cottage. Everyone, including Mark, who hadn't finished his job in the region yet, waited for them with a celebratory feast. Kate and Diane had let the men fire the barbecue, and they took care of the salads and cakes.

No one doubted that both Darcy and Nick would welcome a good homemade meal.

As soon as Nick had called to tell them that he started the drive up the mountain, the men put the steaks onto the grill, and the women began setting the picnic table.

Practically, Nick had lived in Darcy's hospital room for an entire week, so, once he parked his car in the ranch yard and got out, he breathed deeply. For a week, he had left Darcy's side only to make a few trips in town and buy food because what the hospital offered didn't agree either with Darcy or with him.

The man hadn't worried about his horses because he trusted Ryan and Adam to take care of his stud. However, he had missed the mountain air and the quiet atmosphere of his ranch.

Nick helped Darcy out of the car, and then, he slid his arm around her to lead her to the picnic table. Darcy had recovered nicely, and she didn't look like death warmed over anymore. Still, the doctor had prescribed a lot of rest, and Nick was determined to see that she got just that.

Sometimes, Nick read sadness in the woman's eyes, and his heart cringed. He knew that Darcy was thinking of her mother then.

Nick had already given her the news about Wanda's arrest. He hadn't believed that Darcy should be kept in the dark but had waited until he considered that she had recovered enough to withstand such news.

Once Darcy sat down, the guys took turns kissing her cheeks, exasperating Nick with their show of affection.

"All right, all right," he snapped in the end. "Enough is enough," he chased Mark away when the man tried to kiss her a third time. "She needs air, people. I didn't bring her home from the hospital to be smothered to death," Nick glowered at Mark but didn't forget to pierce Ryan and Adam with thunderous eyes as well.

The men laughed at him and thumped him on the back. Ryan didn't miss the occasion to notice, "Well, now, you see how it is to be on the other side. Do you remember when you complained that I was too jealous?"

Kate made an attempt to shush her husband, but he waved her away, determined to have his say.

"No, Kate, I have the right to pay him back. Nick harped on me enough when we were in Malaysia. Well, it's my turn now, and I won't miss my chance," he nodded with conviction.

Nick lost his patience and showed Ryan his finger. Everyone laughed, but Darcy reached out at Nick and intertwined her fingers with his.

She pulled him next to her on the bench, but she knew that she wouldn't have had the strength to make Nick listen to her. However, the man didn't fight her. He immediately sat down, leaning over her.

"Are you all right, baby?" he whispered to Darcy.

She nodded and said quietly, "I am, and you needn't quarrel with your friends. They're just joking with you."

"No, they want to rile me," he retorted and glanced at the men, who had returned to the barbecue.

They had fished a beer bottle each, and now they were flipping the steaks, talking, and laughing. Nick was sure that they were still making fun of him because the guys kept glancing at him with broad grins on their faces.

"Don't pay attention to them," Kate said to Nick, patting his arm. "Sometimes, I have the feeling that men are just big children."

"No, really?" Nick inquired sardonically. He took the longneck beer bottle that Diane put in front of him and took a mouthful.

"Sorry," Kate burst into laughter. "I forgot to mention that I didn't mean you too."

Nick glanced at her askance, wiped his mouth, and said, "I wouldn't have believed you anyway."

"That's because you're smart," Diane observed, smiling at Nick.

"Why is he smart?" Adam inquired, placing a platter with steaks in the middle of the table.

"Yes, why?" Ryan echoed his friend's question, taking the seat next to Kate.

"It doesn't matter," Kate said quickly. "Let's eat. I'm starving," she waved her hand, hoping to make Ryan forget about the discussion.

"No, honey cup, not so fast. I've got the feeling that you were talking about us, and Adam, Mark, and I weren't included in that smart group," Ryan refused to back down.

"Don't worry, we were all included in the same group," Nick said in a dry tone of voice. "But Kate is right. Let's eat. I'm sick and tired of burgers with fries. If I don't see another one for a year, I'll be happy," he added, and immediately filled Darcy's plate with food.

The woman's eyes rounded, and her lips parted when she saw the little mountain that Nick had built on her plate.

"Nick, you're kidding. I might be somewhat round, but I can't eat so much," Darcy tugged at the sleeve of Nick's shirt.

"Who the hell told you that you're round?" Nick snapped. "You look perfect," he said, and his eyes swept over her body appreciatively.

"Thank you," she replied dryly. "Still, I can't eat so much," she repeated stubbornly. Nick's eyebrows bunched on his forehead, and Adam intervened immediately. He felt that his friend might say something that would send him to the dog's house for the night. "Eat as much as you can. You can leave the rest on the plate, Darcy. It's not a problem. I'm sure Nick can finish it. He doesn't only look like a bear. He also has a bear's appetite," he noted with a huge grin on his lips.

Nick dismissed Adam with a rude gesture and turned to Darcy, "Sweetie, just eat."

Reluctantly, Darcy took the fork and started digging into the pile of food under Nick's attentive eyes. Ryan and Adam glanced at each other, and they shook their heads. Kate put her hand on Ryan's knee to stop him from making any comment and invited everyone to help themselves.

After taking a few satisfying bites from his steak, Nick looked straight to Mark and asked, "So, what is the verdict?"

Mark wiped his mouth with a napkin and then braced his elbows on the table.

"We've arrested a few high-placed individuals, including your mother's boyfriend," he turned to Darcy. "I'm sorry, but your mother was also involved in their business. She hadn't been involved for long, just a couple of weeks, but we still can't let her go," he said and leveled his pale green eyes squarely on her.

"I understand," Darcy replied quietly, and her face became scarlet because of the embarrassment.

"It's not your fault," Nick took her hand and squeezed it tenderly. "What your mother has done doesn't define you."

Darcy nodded, but she didn't seem convinced. She felt Nick's eyes lingering on her, so she cut another piece of meat, even though her appetite had vanished.

"Driscoll was the head of the network," Mark continued.

"You know you can talk and still eat," Adam informed him with a wave of his hand toward Mark's steak, which was getting cold. "I'm sure Nick didn't want to deprive you of your food. He wanted some information and a bit of conversation."

Mark thundered Adam with his eyes, but the man just grinned and stuffed his mouth with another piece of his juicy steak.

Mark sighed. He knew Adam well and was accustomed to his insolent behavior, so he didn't bother to say anything to him. Mark reached for his fork and knife again. It would have been a pity indeed to let such a good steak go to waste.

"Driscoll had been hurt pretty badly," Mark mentioned in between bites. "We checked the guns, and girls, you all took a shot at him," he bobbed his brows.

"We didn't have a choice," Diane said haughtily.

"I didn't accuse but praised," Mark said, straightening Diane's skewed perspective.

"Anyway, you really did an excellent job on that huge guy. The Scandinavian-Indian man. The doc said that he would survive in the end, although I don't know how much good would that do to him. From what we found out from Darren, the women, and children we freed, he will never leave the prison," Mark shook his head.

"Oh, Darren," Darcy said. "He's still alive then."

"Yes," Ryan confirmed. "We didn't think that he'd survive, but he proved all of us wrong."

"Why so interested in Darren?" Nick asked, not very happy that Darcy inquired about the man.

"He actually saved both Kate and me. When we finished the bullets, Darren interceded between the attackers and us. That way, we could get into the bedroom and escape," Darcy explained patiently, although Nick's jealousy didn't sit well with her.

"Don't worry so much," Kate reassured Darcy, touching her hand. "I had the same thoughts about Ryan, and in the end, everything turned out quite well. They're just alpha guys and don't like any competition."

Stunned, Darcy looked at Kate with wide eyes. She hadn't thought that she was so transparent or that Kate's abilities were thus developed.

Mark was even more astonished. He couldn't read anything of the kind on Darcy's face, so he frowned.

"Oh, you don't know, Mark," Diane exclaimed. "The guys have probably forgotten to tell you, but Kate can read minds."

"What can Kate do?" Mark shouted with bewilderment.

"Minds, Mark," Ryan answered in a bored tone of voice. "My wife can read your mind if she wants."

"Actually, she did read his mind," Adam interfered, tapping his finger onto the top of the table. "Remember? Malaysia?" he tilted his head. Ryan and Nick nodded.

"What the heck are you talking about?" Mark snapped.

"Kate has the gift of reading minds. There are people like that, and you know it," Nick pointed out. "The best thing is that Kate can read your mind even if she's not next to you."

Mark shook his head, "Unbelievable."

"Anyway, we've moved away from the subject of discussion," Nick pointed his fork to Mark.

The man looked at Nick, nonplussed. "And what was the subject? You shocked me, so I forgot," he admitted.

The three women smiled while Adam rolled his eyes. Ryan didn't want to alienate Mark for good, so he replied patiently, "You were talking about Darren."

"He'll make it. He won't be able to work for a month or two, unfortunately, and I understand he doesn't really have the means to support himself for such a long period, but... I can't help him there."

"So, he won't be indicted," Kate concluded.

"No, he won't. His involvement in human trafficking was minimal. Darren also didn't want to get involved in Driscoll's plan for kidnapping Darcy and killing Nick.

"Darren can come and recover here," Nick said quietly. "The man saved Darcy's life, so that's the least I can do," Nick shrugged.

"If Darren wants, he can work for me afterward. I'd like to spend more time with Darcy if she accepts to remain here with me," he turned to Darcy and took her hand in his, watching her inquiringly.

"Do you want me to stay?" Darcy asked him in a small voice and trained her cobalt eyes on Nick. "For how long?"

Darcy didn't hope too much, but she would have liked to have more time with Nick. The man aroused feelings she had never had, and she felt an intense connection with him.

Unaware that everyone was watching him breathlessly, Nick took her hand and played with her fingers for a few seconds. He brushed his lips over Darcy's knuckles and then gazed straight into her eyes.

"I told you that I love you, and I've never said that to any other woman before. I know what I want, and I want you. Not only for today or tonight, but for the rest of my life."

Darcy's fingers shook in his hand, and she licked her suddenly dry lips. Her other hand tightened on the edge of the table, and she closed her eyes for a few seconds. Then, she gazed at Nick again and asked, "What do you want to say?"

"Not much. Just that I want you to be mine, my wife. And before the month's end," Nick said in a determined tone of voice.

Kate's lips parted, and a sigh flew off her lips. She reached out to Ryan and caught his hand. The man squeezed her hand reassuringly, and then put his thumb in the air, showing to Nick that he approved of his decision.

Diane's eyes filled with tears, and she pressed a hand to her mouth. Adam gathered her gently to his chest, and taking advantage of his position next to Nick, he thumped him on the back and bobbed his head in agreement with his friend's choice.

"Well done, brother," Adam said with a broad grin on his lips.

Only Darcy and Mark stared at Nick wide-eyed. Mark had been in the process to bring the fork to his mouth, and his hand had frozen mid-air when he heard Nick's words.

Mark had known Nick for many years, and he always considered that the man was well-balanced and never made rushed decisions. He couldn't believe his ears and just stared stone-faced at his friend.

Ryan and Adam watched Mark and grinned. They had never had the chance to see the man nonplussed and enjoyed the show.

Nick didn't pay attention to anyone. He just kept staring at Darcy. "I see that you're thrilled with my proposal," he remarked dryly, but regret shone in his eyes.

"No, no, no," Darcy rushed to say and shook her head. "You just left me speechless. I didn't expect that you would propose," she explained, and her words tumbled one after another.

"I tell you that I love you and I want you to live with me. What the heck did you think I meant?" Nick snapped, wanting to cover his gaucherie.

"I don't know," Darcy confessed. "But I didn't think you'd want to marry me."

"I do and soon. What do you say?" Nick insisted.

"I'd love to," Darcy replied, but her eyes still searched the man's face to make sure that she didn't misunderstand.

"Good then," Nick said. "At the end of September then. Is it enough time for you to get used to the idea of being my wife?"

Kate shook her head and rolled her eyes. '*Not even one of these three guys have an ounce of romance in his bones,*' she reflected.

Diane just wiped her tears and smiled. Those men might not have been romantic, but each one of them turned out being the perfect half.

EPILOGUE

THE LAST WEEK OF SEPTEMBER came with rain and wind. Still, that didn't ruin Darcy's and Nick's wedding. Fate smiled upon them, and the sun shone timidly on their wedding day. They held the ceremony on a meadow near the cottage, surrounded by their friends.

Ryan had flown Jeanne and the children to Montana, and Darren had just left the hospital.

The man couldn't believe his luck that he had a roof over his head and prospects for a job once he recovered completely. Nick kept his word and offered Darren the barrack next to the stables.

The pastor who pronounced Nick and Darcy man and wife was astonished to see that Darren and the twins were the only guests. The other three couples were part of the wedding party.

Nick had insisted that Ryan, Adam, and Mark should stand on his side, like groomsmen. Therefore, Darcy chose Kate and Diane as matrons of honor and Jeanne as a bridesmaid.

Nick waited for Darcy's arrival impatiently. Ryan and Adam didn't miss their opportunity to remind him of everything he had said to them when they got married. Mark still had difficulties in understanding the change in Nick. He kept staring at the man and shaking his head.

When Darcy appeared in the distance, Nick rubbed his hands off his dress pants. The woman's ebony hair flew in the wind, beaconing at him. To everyone's astonishment, Nick broke into a run. He didn't stop until he reached Darcy. He didn't care about his friends' shouts and laughter, or about the pastor's disapproving shake of the head.

Nick took Darcy's hands in his and gazed deeply into her cobalt eyes. He leaned over, touched his forehead to hers, and sighed deeply.

"Let's make you mine," he whispered.

Darcy drew back and smiled at him. "Let's do that," she said.

Nick took her hand and brushed his lips of Darcy's knuckles. Then, he said with a resolute tone of voice, "Let's make it faster."

He scooped her in his arms and strode toward the pastor with gigantic strides. Darcy laughed and knotted her fingers behind his neck.

"This is faster indeed," she admitted.

AUTHOR'S BIO

Rowena Dawn writes romance, reads thrillers, and watches comedies. She likes walking through the woods but insanely loves the sea.

She has a love-hate relationship with her writing and drives her dog crazy whenever she doesn't stop writing to take him out.

Table of Contents

PULLED IN

This series *Perfect Halves* will have four books and all of them will be about love, adventure and conspiracies.

Look for Book Four in Rowena Dawn's "*Perfect Halves*" series: **CATCHING LILY – LIVE WIRE.**

Also by Rowena Dawn:

Double-Edged – Book One in The Perfect Halves Series – eBook, paperback, audio book

Eyes in the Dark - Book Two in The Perfect Halves Series – eBook, paperback

Pulled In - Book Three in The Perfect Halves Series – eBook, paperback

Catching Lily – Live Wire – Book Four in the Perfect Halves Series & The Winstons Series – eBook, paperback

Leap of Faith – eBook, paperback, audio book

Becka's Awakening (Book One in The Winstons Series) – eBook, paperback and audio book

Matt's Dilemma (Book Two in The Winstons Series) – eBook, paperback

Mr. (Almost) Right eBook, paperback and audio book

Jay's Salvation (Book Three in The Winstons Series) – eBook, paperback

PULLED IN

Thank you for taking the time to read **PULLED IN**, the third book in the series *The Perfect Halves*.

If you enjoyed it, please consider telling your friends or posting a short review.

Word of mouth is an author's best friend and much appreciated. Thank you,

Rowena Dawn

Don't miss out!

Visit the website below and you can sign up to receive emails whenever Rowena Dawn publishes a new book. There's no charge and no obligation.

https://books2read.com/r/B-A-SAED-THYU

BOOKS 2 READ

Connecting independent readers to independent writers.

Did you love *Pulled In*? Then you should read *Catching Lily -Live Wire*[1] by Rowena Dawn!

[2]

Lily has almost given up on her happily ever after. Mark is just on the run and hopes to keep his hide intact.

A chance encounter makes Lily hope again, and Mark find his stopping point.

Lily comes from a family of witches, and she has got a curse over her head. The Winston family is large, full of wonders, happiness, but also bitterness. Mark is her chance to get involved with a man who resembles no one she has ever known.

---

1. https://books2read.com/u/47EMeN

2. https://books2read.com/u/47EMeN

He is a strong man, full of secrets, and almost cold-hearted. Mark seizes his chance with Lily, but two questions remain to be answered. Will his past chase her away? Will her family secret come between the two of them? Lily and Mark bring together the characters of two romance series, infusing their lives both with suspense and paranormal.

About the Publisher

It is based in Toronto and brings to public various books: poems, novels, short-stories, children's books, language study books and non-fiction. It publishes the literary review: Scarlet Leaf Review: www.scarletleafreview.com

Our mission is to help emerging authors and poets to make their works known to the public.

Contact email address: scarletleafpublishinghouse@gmail.com